Low Down

Tonja Ayers

LOW DOWN

BY

TONJA AYERS

Library of Congress: 2021910480

ISBN-13: 979-8-506-62278-9

Cover design:	Dynasty Covers
Edited:	Gloria Palmer Walker
Proofread & Typeset:	Gloria Palmer Walker
	(movinonup57@yahoo.com)

Published by:

The Shoe Lady Publishing
c/o Emperial Publishing
P.O. Box 21402
Detroit, MI 48221
(313) 449-8543
Website: www.EmperialPub.com

First printing June 2021

Dedication

I usually acknowledge both of my parents, but this time I would like to specifically dedicate this project to my father, Mr. Charlie Ayers Jr., who passed away shortly before the completion of this book.

Thank you, Daddy,
for always loving, supporting, and believing in me.
I thank God for blessing me with you. I love and miss you so much. Some days the pain of living without you is unbearable, but you taught me to be strong and I'm trying my best to do that.
I can't wait to see you again and I hope I'm making you proud.

P.S.: Mama, you know I love you too! Lol

Table of Contents

Low Down

Prologue

Jalen Ross had been gone now for three years and there was about one week left before he would be returning to the gritty streets of the Motor city. Detroit, Michigan, is an 'eat-or-get-eaten' type of city, where only the strong survive in the concrete jungle, and Jalen knew how to survive. He also knew the evidence against him wasn't real, but it still had managed to get him convicted of a felony.

Jalen had been around the block once or twice in his lifetime, but he couldn't figure out who wanted to get rid of him or why. He didn't have any idea of who would stoop that low, but it was obvious someone had wanted him off the streets and out of the way. Now that he had finally gotten his freedom back, he was going to find out somehow, someway, who was behind this set up and they would pay dearly. If he ended up in jail again, it would be rightfully so.

Jail is a messed-up place, and it wasn't a place he would wish on his worst enemy. No one wanted to do time and definitely not for a crime they hadn't committed, especially for a sex crime against a child. Fortunately, Jalen hadn't suffered the wrath of sexual assault like many men do when incarcerated for raping a child, and he often wondered if he had a guardian angel in prison.

Jackson State Penitentiary was soon to be in Jalen's past and he would finally be back home with his beautiful wife, Taylor. Jalen sat on his bunk, making sure his cellmate wasn't watching him as he reread the letter that had arrived for him today during mail call. He had a nosy-ass cellmate who never received mail or visits, and because of that, he got on Jalen's nerves every day. For someone to be doing life in the joint, Jalen figured he should be in chill mode and acclimated to his forever surroundings by now, but this dude was always running around like the Energizer Bunny. When Jalen figured Mr. Nosy was good and distracted, he started reading the letter again.

Jalen,

I can't wait for you to be free again. I have counted each and every day. I have been so lonely these past 36 months without you being here when I needed you. I know you probably won't believe it, but I have actually been counting down the days. I also downloaded a countdown app on my phone. Lol

I have some good news! I received a promotion yesterday. I am officially a sergeant in the Detroit Police Department! Can you believe that, baby? Now I'll be able to ride around in a squad car alone. I can't wait to pull you over and frisk you. Lol

The streets have been very busy lately with elections coming up and crime not slowing down. We're pressured to 'clean up the city' when election season approaches, and guess who decided to give up their seat on the city council and run for mayor? Ya boy, Grant Ashford! You know how much I can't stand that man. Well, I'm going to keep this one brief and short. I can't wait to see you and I miss those big juicy lips all over me. Love you!

You know who.

"Hey, man, what you down there reading? You got to be the only person I know who gets mail just days before their release date," his cellmate looked over the top bunk and said before jumping down.

"Just a letter from my wife, man, telling a brother she can't wait to see him and shit like that. You know how women are," Jalen lied, being a little sarcastic knowing his cellmate never received any mail. Well, not any personal mail. Most of his mail was legal stuff from his lawyer, who didn't have a chance in hell of winning his appeal.

"Yeah, but you're a lucky dude, because most men going home don't have a wife to go home to," he laughed.

"Lucky? What's that supposed to mean?" Jalen asked.

"There's an old blues song that says, *'Ain't no sense in going home / Jody's got your girl and gone.'* Most men doing time have to try to keep Jody away from their home. I hope you know there's definitely been some man smashing your wife, and if you don't have to worry about a man, then it's her listening to her friends. 'Girl, bye. He in jail. You waitin' on him? Couldn't be me.' I mean sometimes some of these fools get two years out of their women, but not much longer than that." He laughed thinking about his own situation. He had been down for over ten years, and he'd told Jalen his girl had left him six months after he was sentenced.

"Shit, you've been gone three years now. You can bet money Jody has come through your house and gone. She probably wrote you that letter right after he left," he continued, still laughing, but at the same time wishing he had received a letter from someone.

"True, but that was her decision. Even though she's my wife, I wasn't trying to make her do this time with me. If she wanted to bounce, I would have been cool with that. Shit, I thought I was going to be gone for a long time. Any man with an ounce of common sense should understand a woman has needs, and if he really loves his woman, he should love her enough to let her go. If it was the other way around, would you wait on your girl? Hell no!" Jalen exclaimed and chuckled to himself.

"I feel you, bro. You can talk that shit now that you're going home, but don't act like you don't want to know who's been there and done that. On that note, they're about to call Rec time, homie. You want to get one last workout in? Let's see if you can bench as much shit as you talk," his celly said, looking out the small window on the cell door.

"I think I'm going to pass this time, bro. I won't be working out too much more before I'm out this bitch. Right now, I just want to relax and fix me a hook-up. I'm about to eat these noodles and chips. Plus, my baby sent me a new book to read," Jalen said, calmly looking at the back cover.

"Let me see that book. Looks like it might be interesting," his celly said, taking the book out of Jalen's hand.

Jalen didn't like sharing his belongings with other inmates. He had learned when he first came in the joint that these folks were criminals and would do anything to survive. Books in the joint were like having dope out on the streets. Niggas would kill you for a few good paragraphs.

"*The Apple Don't Fall Far From The Tree* sounds like a subliminal message. I think she's trying to tell you something. Is she just like her father or are you just like yours? My bad, do you even know yo' daddy? Ain't never heard you mention him," he continued, laughing again and secretly hating on Jalen.

"Stop hating, bro, and give me my damn book back. Funny thing is, I ain't never seen your ass with nothing but them old-ass rap magazines since we've been cellmates. Can you even read? My bad, were you just lookin' at the pictures?" Jalen playfully said, paying his cellmate back for trying to throw shade all the time.

"Fuck you! I don't know why you would want to stay in this cell, but suit yourself, my man. I don't want to be in this room any longer than I have to. I'll find somebody who can stand this pressure. Holla at you around lunch time," he said, listening for the bars to break.

Once Jalen's cellmate was gone, Jalen put the book down and took the letter from his special friend back out. He reread it again, sniffing the stationary it was written on. The pretty pink letterhead was scented with a sweet fragrance his nose was unfamiliar with, but the scent turned him on. He reminisced about the last time they were together and how his friend had done everything in his power to clear his name, but the powers that be seemed to be strongly set on sending him to prison.

Jalen looked at the last lines of his letter and thought about Grant Ashford, who had been a Detroit city Council member for eight years now. Grant had been Jalen's best-kept secret. Until one day, just like that, Grant had texted him and told him they were finished. It was an unexpected text out of the clear blue, and Jalen had raked his brain over and over again trying to figure out why.

They were madly in love, had meaningful conversations, and the sex between them had been dynamic every time they got together. Jalen had no idea what had prompted Grant's breakup of their secret, down-low love affair. They *both* were married and they *both* had an established set of rules which neither one of them had ever broken.

That was what was so puzzling to Jalen. Even though he'd accepted Grant's decision, he really cared about Grant Ashford, almost like come-out-the-closet-type caring. He was glad he hadn't come clean with his wife, and that Grant had done what he'd done before Jalen had ruined his situation with not just his wife but a few other people who wouldn't have taken it well either. If that had happened, he wouldn't have a place to go home to and Grant would be living his life as if nothing ever had happened.

Jalen knew Grant had a son whom he truly loved, and Jalen didn't have any children. His wife was too busy working and had neither the time nor the desire to raise children. Jalen admired Grant's relationship with his son and often dreamt of having his own family one day. Grant always mentioned how he would feel if his son found out about his private lifestyle, and Jalen understood that wholeheartedly. They had nothing but love and respect for each other, so Jalen knew Grant's family wasn't the problem either. Nothing had changed since they'd started having their affair, nothing but Grant's mind.

Now wasn't the time for him to worry or think about Grant Ashford; that was over and done with. He always felt the best way to get over one man was to get on top of another one, and he'd managed to do just that. He smiled reading the letter again and again.

Jalen's thoughts drifted from his special friend to his wife and going home to her. He wondered if he still wanted to be married, and if, in fact, being on the 'down low' was the worst sin a man could commit toward a woman. Was being on the "down low" really just being "low down"? Jalen had stopped praying a long time ago because he felt he had become a convicted felon because he had been deceiving one of God's children.

It was his life and he knew he had choices. He also knew those choices had consequences, but he liked the down-low lifestyle because it came with risks and those risks got him many rewards, like money, watches, season tickets to sports events, and vacations. Occasionally, when he was with Grant, he would get a plane ticket to meet in Washington, D.C. or some incredible place. He remembered the first time he'd seen the White House; it had been amazing. What was even more amazing was that it was in the hood with a whole project unit just a few blocks away behind the Oval Office. That was some of the stuff he missed about Grant—the enlightening conversations and new experiences they'd shared when spending time together.

Jalen's wife, Taylor, was exceptionally beautiful, and she deserved a man who would be real with her. It was just so easy for Jalen to be two people and never worry about her finding out about his other life and the lifestyle he lived. She was so involved in the church and the church's business that her whole life was centered around New Covenant Baptist Church. Her father, Pastor Burk, had grown a huge following, one of the largest followings in Detroit, and she handled everything for him except the sermon on Sundays.

The church kept her busy seven days a week. Monday was ladies' night, Tuesday was children's Bible study, and Wednesday was adult Bible study, twice a day. Thursday was men's fellowship day. Jalen didn't understand why her father wanted her there then, but she was always required to be there. Friday was board meetings, and Saturday was choir rehearsal and meetings, mostly about financial investment of the church's money.

As far as Jalen was concerned, he felt Pastor Burk was investing the money his own way. He'd purchased the Bishop's Mansion from the Detroit Piston's John Salley years ago after Salley left

Detroit. The home had fourteen bedrooms. Who in the hell needs fourteen bedrooms? The pastor also had two Bentleys and a Cadillac Escalade, which he traded in for the latest model every other year. He also had two sports cars tucked away at his five thousand-square-foot home with the six-car garage. Jalen thought he was traveling better than Jesus ever traveled.

It was "church business" that had kept Taylor from handling her own personal business the correct way at home. Jalen had warned her several times that he needed attention from her, and Taylor always said she would be more mindful of his needs. That hadn't happened, and to this day, Taylor was still taking care of the church's business.

When he made up his mind being faithful was out the window, Jalen didn't know what his plan was going to be. He was extremely good looking, slim but in great physical shape, and could have any woman he wanted. Jalen was a popular party promoter in Detroit and he could have easily finessed a female bar or club owner he worked with to give up some sex, but he'd learned at a young age not to stick his dick in the cash register, as his father would say.

Jalen's father, Jackson, however, was better at giving advice than he was at following it. Jalen's mother, Charlene, had caught his father cheating with his female boss and had shot them multiple times, killing them both. She had literally snapped and lost her mind. She was serving natural life in jail, and her actions had caused Jalen, an only child, to be left all alone. It was his fear of loneliness which had caused Jalen to step out on his wife.

First, it was the strip clubs for Jalen, but that became too expensive, then a couple of times, he'd picked up a few stray hookers who looked like they were hustling to get high. He began thinking that was way too risky and he tried to maintain a few outside relationships, but none of the women were in the position to take care of him financially the way Taylor did. He had to admit though, he missed the riskiness of picking up streetwalkers. It was cheaper than the strip club and less time-consuming than trying to juggle two relationships, but that decision was how all his drama had started.

Jalen's last pick-up on the streets had changed him permanently. The day he picked up Viola Reaves had altered Jalen's life forever and he would never be the same man.

Viola was taller than your average woman, with curves and long, toned legs that most women would envy. Jalen was cruising up Woodward Avenue near 6 Mile Road in Detroit, when he saw her in a short, tight mini-skirt and decided to pull over. She sashayed toward his truck wearing platform stilettoes, and after a few minutes of casual chit-chat, Viola got in Jalen's white Range Rover smelling like she lived in the perfume section at Macy's department store. She was sassy, and Jalen knew she was going to be a handful.

Jalen had tried calling his wife Taylor about an hour ago, but her phone had kept going straight to voicemail, so he already knew what that meant. Her ringer was turned off because she was handling "church business". He was horny and livid that Taylor was at church when he was ready to relieve himself after planning and hosting a long, stressful day party, so he decided he would just make a friendly purchase from some woman on the streets. Taylor never drove his truck, so he stayed prepared by keeping a locked glove compartment full of condoms and wipes just in case he needed them.

Viola was the first woman to catch his eye when he hit the stroll, and when he saw those curves, he knew he had to have her. Jalen headed north on Woodward Avenue, made the turn around, and pulled into Palmer Park, about half a mile from where he'd picked Viola up. He found a secluded area where no one was around and pulled the truck over. He was looking at her ruby red lips and became anxious to get his jeans down around his ankles. After sizing her up, he knew the head would be good, but when he wanted to fuck, he would have to lay the seat all the way back and have her straddle him with her head sticking up through the sunroof.

"You aren't a violent man, are you?" Viola asked, displaying a diminutive smile.

"I don't know. If you consider being horny violent, then I might be a serial killer," Jalen said jokingly, reaching to grab one of Viola's breasts. He could see her nipples through her sheer shirt. They were large and soft, and he started to stroke his manhood through his pants after touching her.

"I have to tell you something before we get this party started. I like being honest. I don't want any problems," Viola stated.

Jalen was thinking, *'Oh shit, here we go! This bitch has an STD or something.'* It would be just his luck to find someone who was this good looking, just to find out she was contaminated.

"Don't tell me you've got some type of virus. I ain't going for no bullshit like that. Hell muthafuckin no!" he spat seriously.

"No, baby. Trust me, sugah, I ain't infected with anything but love. I just want to let you know something."

"What is it? Shit, if you're clean, everything else can be worked out," Jalen responded, thinking she wanted an extra twenty or something.

"Oh really? I'm glad you said that. I was born a man," Viola confided.

"A MAN! What the fuck?! Get yo' punk ass out my muthafuckin truck!" Jalen said, wondering how this dude had breasts and they were real.

"Well, thanks for having an open mind. I'll get out. Like I said, I don't want any trouble. I just had to be honest with you," Viola said, opening the door, about to get out.

Jalen was shocked he had picked up a man. He was even more shocked that he couldn't tell Viola *was* a man. They both had the same instrument between their legs, but here this muthafucka was out here posing as a woman. Several thoughts went through his mind, but the one he couldn't shake was knowing someone had to be picking Viola up for him/her to still be out there.

He wondered what it would be like get head from a man. He had a friend who was a lesbian and she always told him that a man could never do to a woman what another woman could do. Now he wondered if that same theory held true for men. Could Viola give him some satisfaction that Taylor had no idea how to achieve?

He looked around and knew they were somewhere no one could see them. They were tucked away inside Palmer Park, and even though the 12th Police Precinct was less than a mile away, everyone knew the police rarely patrolled the park.

"Hey, wait a minute. You're pretty far from the stroll. How're you gonna get back?" Jalen asked, stopping Viola.

"I don't know. Guess I'll have to walk, but I'll make it," Viola replied flatly.

"Come on, get back in. I ain't going to be like that," he replied, not believing he was having second thoughts about letting a tranny touch him. But it served Taylor right for always being busy and not tending to his needs. He figured he could try it just this one time since no one would know.

Viola fixed her wig and adjusted her breasts when she sat back in his passenger seat. Jalen quickly unzipped his zipper and she/he went to work on him. He had to admit it was extraordinary, ten times better than Taylor's head game, and to this day, it was the best oral sex he had ever received. Viola had him shaking and his toes curling in his shoes. He moaned, oohed, and ahhed, digging his nails into her back as she got to work. He got so excited, he almost pulled her wig off.

That's when Viola came up for air and purred, "Hands off the hair, daddy, unless you're paying for a new wig."

Jalen liked her sassiness and continued to let her service him. Viola was the first time in his life he'd ever ejaculated from oral sex and it wouldn't be his last.

After that day, he made it his business to meet up with Viola a few times a week. He was hooked like a crackhead. It started off as just oral sex and Jalen had no problem with that because Viola loved to swallow his juices, but soon, things escalated to more sexually-explicit meetings. Jalen became what some call a "top". He penetrated Viola anally, but he was never penetrated, which in his mind did not make him "gay". Viola and Jalen spent a lot of time together, and even went out occasionally for dinner to places in surrounding counties so they wouldn't be seen by anyone they knew.

That was almost four years ago, and every now and then, he would think about Viola Reaves, also known as Victor Bennett. His life had moved in different directions since Victor, but he'd continued to see male friends. They had never turned into anything serious, then Jalen had decided to raise his standards and began to pursue an upper echelon of men who had no choice but to keep their secrets. When playing this game, you must deal with someone who has just as much or more to lose than you do. That was how he'd met Grant Ashford, his first big fish as he liked to called him. At first, it was a money and power thing for Jalen, but he eventually fell in love with Grant.

Jalen finished writing his letter to his special friend and decided to write his wife a letter as well. The time for him to see her face-to-face was coming soon, and if it wasn't for the financial benefit, he would ask Taylor for a divorce his first day home.

Chapter I

October 1st...

There was one month left before the election, and Grant Ashford was in his office thinking about the move he was going to make. For the last eight years, he had been satisfied with his position as a councilman for the city of Detroit. He'd never wanted to move up the ladder to face the problems the previous black mayors had had to face. Grant knew he would be challenged with every decision when it came to spending the city's money trying to improve the quality of life in Detroit.

The automotive industry had been in deep trouble. President Obama's bail out had helped and things were better, but not good. In the sixties and seventies, thousands of people had migrated from the South to Detroit to make a living, but now the population was steadily declining as Detroit residents moved back down South in search of employment and economic security. Grant reached over and hit the intercom button linked to his secretary's desk.

"Yes, boss," Vanessa responded.

Vanessa Jones had been Grant's secretary for this last term. She was a young woman who'd graduated from the University of Michigan with a degree in criminal justice. He knew her goal was to pursue her major and open her own law firm, so he was grateful to have had her as long as he had.

"Come in here for a second please. I need you to look over this speech. I don't know if it's on-point," he said, admiring her skills with words. She was truly a wordsmith.

"Not a problem, boss," she responded. "Just give me one second. I was going over the newly-suggested budget cuts for the public school system."

Vanessa was a lifesaver at times. Grant knew she had a thing for him, but neither of them had the audacity to act upon it—Vanessa because she didn't want to lose her job if it didn't work out, and Grant because he was married and had a family. Besides, the city had seen enough scandal with political relationships in Detroit. He wasn't going to be next in line to deal with that mess.

She walked into his office wearing a nice, professional but fitted skirt and a white blouse. Vanessa had nice legs and a shape like she worked out every day, maybe even twice a day.

She always wore her shirts open and displayed just enough cleavage to cause a sensual arousal in most men. That was one thing he had to ignore if he was going to continue to not cross the line with her. Vanessa's cappuccino complexion and short, stylish pixie haircut made her very attractive. With all that beauty and the right attributes, Grant still had managed to keep their relationship one hundred percent professional.

She had a way of invading his personal space and she stood alongside him instead of in front of his desk as she read the speech he had prepared. *Fox News* was doing a segment tomorrow on both candidates running for the mayoral seat, and he wanted to sound like he knew what he was talking about. Grant knew for sure he was going to win. It had been promised to him from a higher source, that if he ran, he would definitely be victorious in the mayoral election.

"Okay, boss, this is good. I think you need to address the gentrification concerns and talk more about the micro and macro fixtures you plan to implement to make a change," she said, walking around to the front of his desk and leaning slightly over it to hand him back his iPad. He knew she was doing it again, and he was pretty close to reacting since he hadn't had a chance to see his boo last night.

He'd settled for a nightcap with his wife Ava instead, who he had been married to for twenty years. They had a son who was away in college studying medicine with the goal of becoming a doctor. Ava was a good woman at heart, but to him, she was too much of a social butterfly. She was very materialistic and expensive to take care of. Nothing for her was normal; if it was, she didn't want it. HIGH END was even on her license plates. She got on his last nerve at times, and even though he genuinely loved her to pieces, he just didn't know how much he was *in love* with her. Divorce in his family was unheard of, and in reality, she didn't do anything to warrant him seeking one. Spending money like they were Jay-Z and Beyoncé didn't warrant him asking for a divorce. Although that was Nick Cannon's reason for divorcing Mariah Carey, they were celebrities and people expected them to spend lavishly. Ava just wanted to floss around the streets of Detroit.

Grant watched his secretary sashay out his office back to her office, thinking, *'There goes a nice piece of ass.'* It was a true statement, but it just wasn't for him. He looked back at his speech, wondering where he was going to tweak it and add some of the things she was talking about, which to him made a lot of sense. Grant loved his city and wanted to rejuvenate his hometown by importing new businesses to decrease the unemployment rate and also to create affordable housing.

His city had once been home to millions of people; now, some parts of Detroit looked like a war-torn, third-world country. Many businesses had packed up and moved to the suburbs or outsourced jobs overseas. A few major corporations like Compuware and Quicken Loans had relocated to downtown Detroit, but Grant wanted to focus on rebuilding the neighborhoods.

Just as he was in deep thought, his personal cellphone started ringing in his jacket pocket. When he looked at the Caller ID, Walter's name showed up. He quickly sent the call to voicemail because he didn't have time to speak to the governor at the moment. He made a mental note to call him back when he left the office in a few minutes. Grant knew he would get an earful because Walter hated to be sent to voicemail, but timing was everything in life, especially in his life.

Chapter 2

It was still early in the season and the Detroit Lions looked a lot better this year than they had the year before. They had made a few trades and brought in some help on both the defensive and offensive ends, which made them true contenders for their division. Coach Addison was happy with what was going on out on the field, and he was even more satisfied with what was going on off the field in his personal life as well.

This Sunday was a very big game, probably one of the biggest games of the regular season for his team. The Lions were playing their number-one rival, the Green Bay Packers, who were a game-and-a-half ahead as of right now. After beating their number-two rival, the Minnesota Vikings, the fans were hoping for another division win, and Coach Michael Addison wanted the exact same thing. Not only would it clinch a playoff spot, but it would make him look like a hero by taking the Lions to the playoffs his first year as head coach. A winning team is job security within the NFL.

The game wasn't the only big thing transpiring this Sunday at the stadium. Instead of a regular halftime show, the stadium was going to be home to the first mayoral electoral speech. A local election speech being broadcast to millions of viewers is pretty much unheard of, but this candidate was known for dancing to the beat of his own drum. Walter had a connect at *Fox News* who had arranged the whole thing. Grant Ashford, a Detroit native and graduate of Harvard University, was going to be speaking during the halftime show. He would be giving the most-important speech of his campaign run on the fifty-yard line. There had been a lot of buzz about him running for the position, like he had already won it, and Michael had a feeling Grant was going to win. It was being talked about at parties and in private emails only certain people who were privy could view. Michael surely knew most of the important people, and that was how word had gotten back to him.

Coach Addison had made a conscious effort to avoid situations that had Grant Ashford attached to them. He had a different perspective about Grant Ashford, the councilman. Sunday wasn't going to be their first ride at the rodeo together, and Michael Addison had not only seen Grant's first show many years ago, but he had been the steer that had gotten away. That memory was from a long time ago but remained a constant reminder of the games people played with your feelings.

When Michael Addison found out Grant Ashford was a councilman in Detroit, he almost hadn't accepted the job as head coach for the team. He had been coaching in Baltimore for the last four years and was tired of finishing every season with a losing record, in addition to working for a front office that was too cheap to make any changes. As much as he wanted to wash away memories of Grant Ashford, he was about to be forced to rehash the harsh moments of their reality. Grant could have been a great football player had he chosen to pursue his athletic career.

Michael had loved Grant's passing game. The young Grant had had an arm on him that could throw the ball almost the entire length of the field and hit his target square in the chest. A *Hail Mary* is a long forward pass, and back in his day, he had been known as the *Hail Mary King.* The league still hadn't seen an arm like his since. It was a shame he hadn't been wise enough to separate his personal life from his professional life, but Michael knew Grant had been young back then and not quite as polished as he looked to be now. Politics wasn't a bad choice for Grant, and Michael could see him prospering while playing in a field full of liars and deceivers.

Sunday was still going to be a moment he dreaded. Michael had hoped, that even though he and Grant Ashford were in the same city, they would never have to cross paths. The private clubs and secret societies they both belonged to in Detroit were already enough, but he somehow had managed to stay under the radar, avoiding Grant at any event he attended. That was because of the memories; they were still too vivid for Michael at times. When he heard about the speech, he realized, that although many years had passed, he still had feelings for the councilman. He didn't understand how someone who was supposed to love you could just stand right in front of you, look you in your face one day, and blurt out, "It's over!" Just like that—no explanation, no warning—just said it and walked away. "It's over." It was the worst fourth quarter of a game Michael had ever coached in his life.

Crushed and heartbroken at the same damn time didn't feel good, and it had not been an easy thing for him to get over. When Grant had graduated and never looked back, Michael knew his life had to go on. He'd left coaching college at the first opportunity he received, and now here he was, coach of his second professional football team—not only head coach, but the first African American to coach the Detroit Lions.

Michael knew it was beneath him to hold a grudge. He felt people had to let bygones be just that, bygones, and move on with their lives, no matter how much pain it caused. He felt there were some people in his past who would have loved for him to fail, to be somewhere coaching a high school team, and if he hadn't gotten his act together, that very well could have happened.

When Grant had broken it off, Michael had been close to admitting himself to a mental institution, and at one point, he'd turned to using cocaine. He was so distraught, he'd even quit coaching for a year and was on his way to rock bottom, until he'd pulled himself back together and decided to move on with his life.

For the first time in over twenty years, he was going to be in the same building as Grant Ashford. It was funny because Michael and Grant were members of the same golf club and played in the same poker circle, but somehow, Michael had strategically managed to never be in either place if Grant was going to be present. So far, he had been extremely lucky at avoiding his ex-lover. Michael knew he had to pull himself together once again and put on his big-boy boxers, wipe up the mess, and keep it pushing, which was his motto. He'd been teaching his players that for years, and now was the time to follow his own advice. He had a team to coach and a game to win. Fuck the fact that Grant Ashford was going to be in the building.

Practice was just ending, and Coach Addison stood out in the middle of the field, just looking around and admiring the architectural design of the new stadium. He turned around in a complete circle with his eyes closed, thinking about his life and what was possible for his future if he won the playoffs. He smiled as he looked in the sky and headed back toward the locker room to end his day. A few of the players had already dressed out and were standing around. This was what they usually did after a nice workout.

"Hey, Coach, good practice," his tight end said.

"Yeah, man, that was one hell of a workout today. Can't wait until those Green Bay cheese-eating boys show their faces in Motown. We're going to spank that ass!" Jermaine, the defensive back, added.

"Hey, one thing to remember: here in Detroit, we keep that stuff professional," Coach said, sticking his key in his office door.

"Ahhhh shit, Coach. Stop being such a soft ass all the damn time, man. This shit is a contact sport and we get a lot of money to make contact!" Jermaine said, waving his hand in Coach's direction. The rest of the team that were standing nearby laughed.

"Calm down, son. A great man once said, the next time you make it to the end zone, act like you've been there before," Coach replied, closing his office door behind him.

He sat at his desk, leaning back in his leather chair, and stared at the wall. He looked at a life-size picture he had in a frame of Vince Lombardi, who was not just a king of the game, but also an amazing philanthropist who was amazing with words. A few minutes later, he heard a knock at the door, breaking the reverie his mind was lodged in.

"Come in," Coach Addison said, sitting up and not asking who it was before extending the invite. It was his general manager, Brian Harris, who had been with the franchise for a long time. Michael knew Harris wanted his position, but the two of them worked well together nevertheless, and Harris was a great assistant. He probably could have made some team a great coach, it just wasn't going to be the Lions.

"What can I do for you, Hairy?" Michael asked, using Harris' nickname.

"Nothing, Coach. I was just coming to tell you I'm out for the night. You know my wife doesn't drive and I have to take her to her sister's house to gossip. I don't know why they just can't talk on the phone," Brian replied, and they both laughed.

"Sounds like a plan. Is there anyone left out there?"

"Only Billy Mundane, and he just got in the shower a few seconds ago, I think. Can't believe as fast as he is out on the field, he's the slowest man in the locker room," Brian replied, closing the coach's door behind him and heading home to his wife and family.

Billy Mundane was definitely the star of the team this season. He was a great quarterback who was quick on his feet and had a snap release that was almost as good as Grant's had been back in the day. But, Billy just couldn't catch a break. He had always been in a bad situation wherever he went because of his personal problems, which Michael understood better than anyone. They shared some of the same viewpoints, and it was their daily conversations that had made them realize how much they really had in common.

Coach stood up and walked around his desk to head out. He would have to walk right past the showers. Normally, he would have stopped and they would have shared some banter or went for a beer, but this thing with Grant happening Sunday had him in an emotional disarray. He opened his door to try to sneak out, but to his surprise, Billy was standing there with just a towel wrapped around him and nothing else. The water was still beaded on his chest as he pushed the coach back inside his office.

"We're all alone now," Billy said.

Chapter 3

Grant Ashford ended his call with Walter as he pulled into his driveway. Walter wanted to see him, but Grant had already made plans with Ava to go out to dinner this evening. They were expecting their son to return home tomorrow and they wanted to spend some quality time alone before his return.

Grant wished, when Walter wanted to meet, he would give him more of a notice than the last-second shit he always tried pulling. He was grateful for his friend because he knew it was Walter who'd made sure he won his second term as councilman and it would be Walter who made sure he won this mayoral election as well. He never knew how Walter had learned about his private life and who he was with behind closed doors, but dealing with Walter had opened a whole new world for Grant.

Right now, he had a lot on his mind, which was how things had been lately. Grant knew it would be good to sit and share some nice political views and some other conversation with his friend Walter, who was the governor and going for his second re-election as well. Grant was reluctant to enter the mayoral election, but it had been Walter's bright idea for him to run and he was the one who would personally secure his seat in the mayor's office. If there was one thing Walter knew how to do, it was how to get what he wanted, and that also applied to winning elections.

Grant felt his pocket to make sure what he was looking for hadn't fallen out. When he felt it, he took the package out of his inside jacket pocket and opened it again, looking at the pictures inside. The package included pictures of a young girl, rape kit results, and two DNA tests from Burk Laboratories— the key evidence in a trial that had happened three years ago.

Grant had believed Walter had used them to set up an old friend and wanted to say something, but things had gotten complicated and he couldn't take any changes on messing up his career by allowing his personal feelings to cloud his rational thinking. He knew he was wrong, and finally, Grant's conscience had gotten the best of him. He couldn't prove it at first, but his gut had told him to keep looking. He had done some investigating and discovered Walter was behind it, just as he'd thought. So, he pulled some strings, unbeknownst to Walter, to have Jalen's case exonerated. Jalen would be getting released soon, and Grant wondered if his freedom and exoneration would affect his campaign. If nothing else, it would definitely affect his mindset.

He knew Walter would be pissed and he would have to share his actions with him soon, because skeletons are not good for an election. It's best to be proactive when one is aware of a potential scandal. That was the benefit of being friends with Walter. He had power and people in the right places to make things go exactly the way he wanted them to go, but this time, Grant wanted to be included in the decision-making process. Grant no longer had a romantic interest in Jalen. Hopefully, he would just go away and be grateful to be free.

Grant shoved the package into his glove box and locked it, double-checking to make sure it was secure. He made a mental note that they were going to take Ava's car.

The next issue Grant had to address was what was happening on Sunday. He would be giving his speech at halftime during the Lions game at the stadium. Again, that was one of Walter's bright ideas. Walter wanted the speech to be heard by the millions of viewers who watched Sunday football, and he figured what better way than to do it while one of the biggest games of the season was played.

Normally, it would have been a great idea to Grant, but seeing how Michael Addison was now the coach of the team, Grant knew it would bring back a lot of unwanted memories. He had not run into Michael Addison since he had been in town and Grant knew he didn't want to. He figured Michael would go out of his way to avoid contact with him because of how he'd ended things so abruptly with Michael back when they were an item.

Grant was just that type of guy. When he felt someone or something was getting too close, he would abandon the thought and the responsibility of loving another man. Jalen had fallen victim and there were a few other men who'd suffered the consequences when Grant was finished with them. Michael was the first heart he'd broken, but his wasn't the last. It was sometimes cruel, but he would do whatever it took to rid himself of any future dealings.

He turned off his headlights and sat thinking in his car in the driveway for a few minutes, reminiscing on the good and the bad times he had shared with Michael. It was a crazy feeling because Michael had not been at the forefront of his mind in several years. He used to think about the man who was his coach and his lover every night after he'd first walked away from their situation, but he'd figured Michael was living by his own motto: When the milk is spilt, clean it up and move on. It was something like that, he thought and chuckled to himself.

There had almost been a coming-out party for the both of them at one point in their relationship and that was what had scared Grant. Michael was much older than he was, and on top of that, Grant's college sweetheart was carrying his child. Both men thought they were so deeply in love at one point that their careers and future lives didn't matter. When Grant confided in Michael that Ava was pregnant, Michael had offered to pay for her abortion and he told Grant he would also give her ten thousand dollars to go away. At first Grant thought it was a great idea, but he knew it would most likely be his only chance of making another life. Ava was far enough along that her ultrasound revealed she was having a boy. It was that revelation of having a son that made Grant relinquish the thought of what Michael had tried to get him to agree to.

Somehow, Grant was able to back away from his whole ordeal with Michael, not giving him a valid reason for walking out and leaving him hanging. The memory was vivid: Fourth quarter in a game against the Navy and Harvard was down by three. There was less than a minute to go and

Grant's team was faced with fourth and long. He heaved a pass downfield, hitting his receiver square in the chest like he always did, and the player scored. There were still twenty seconds left, and when Grant walked off to let the punting unit on, he walked off the field and out of Michael's life for good. He pulled Michael to the side so none of his teammates could hear what he had to say, which wasn't going to be very much.

"It's over."

That was exactly what he'd said, looking Michael right in his eyes. Michael thought he meant the game for a second, but before he could congratulate Grant on the game-winning pass, Grant was headed for the locker room. No interview with the press, no being carried off the field by his teammates—it was over. Grant left the game, leaving his helmet at Michael's feet, and he ultimately left his chances at becoming a professional football player that day. His breakup with Michael fueled his decision to transfer colleges and pursue a different major, which had led him to a career in political science.

After that day, Grant's life had been one big ball of deceit and lies. All his life, he'd had to cover up his true identity of who he really was and what he needed to make him feel loved.

He'd met Ava Jenkins his sophomore year in college at a party and the two of them had hit it off well. Grant knew he was attracted to men and women, but men were his preference. He didn't want to lead the young beauty queen on at first. He really just wanted a cordial friendship with her, but she kept forcing the issue, and eventually, landed in his off-campus apartment and in his bed. That one night of lovemaking with Ava had changed his whole direction.

The first time he slept with Ava, he hadn't had any condoms and they were already too far into the act for him to run to a store; plus, she'd said she was on birth control. That same night was the night Ava was impregnated with their son. Ava claimed it was a mistake, but in retrospect, Grant knew better than that. She had planned everything from the start. Ava was the type of bon vivant person who knew what she wanted her future to consist of, and she'd seen Grant's bright future before he had. She wasn't taking a chance on not becoming Mrs. Grant Ashford. He'd hoped they would have more children, but his wife hadn't wanted to "put her body through that again," so Grant had had a vasectomy shortly after the birth of their son.

Now he felt stuck, trapped in a world where everything was a façade. His marriage was based on lukewarm love, his career was an alternative to playing football, and being a father was the only thing about his life he actually enjoyed. Grant had learned there was a huge difference between loving someone and being in love with someone. One leaves you yearning to be with a person. You smile when you receive a text message or your heart flutters when you see them. You think about how their day is going, if they're okay, or if they need anything. That's being in love and that was not how Grant felt about Ava. He had love for her, but no passion or urgent desire to be with her, and frankly, Jalen was the last person who'd given him butterflies and made him feel that way.

Grant was now raising a son under the false pretense that he was a heterosexual man, and that wasn't right. He often felt like a hypocrite. How could he raise and teach his son to be comfortable in his own skin when he wasn't comfortable in his? He'd prayed at times for a change, but there weren't going to be any changes to his life that he could see. He was who he was and dealing with that fact was left entirely up to him. Grant had prayed on his situation many nights, asking God for forgiveness, but he also realized God gave every man and woman free will to do what they felt their flesh needed to do, and Grant had chosen his happiness in secrecy.

Finally, after thinking and clearing his mind, Grant felt a little better and decided to walk into his home and get the evening underway with his beautiful wife. He still looked at Ava as a beautiful woman, but Ava didn't deserve him and he knew that. Grant knew he loved her because she was who she was: a woman with a lot of nerve and swag that had been good for his unwanted career. If it weren't for her constant pushing him to do more, he probably wouldn't be the important man he was today. Ava made him think it was true that it was a man's world that would be nothing without a woman's touch. That popular cliché held a lot of weight with Grant Ashford, especially the beginning, *this is a man's world.* He sometimes changed the end to say, it would be nothing if a man didn't touch another man.

"Honey, is that you?" she called from the upper level of their mini-mansion.

"Yes, of course, unless the mailman has a key," he said playfully, but not putting anything past her. Are you ready?" he replied back up the stairs just as a text message came across his phone.

"Give me five minutes, baby. I had to change shoes and now I'm just putting on my lipstick," she responded.

He didn't respond because he knew five minutes meant more like fifteen-to-twenty. They had reservations at her favorite place, but he wasn't worried about being late. His credentials always got him special privileges wherever they went. Grant felt a vibration in his pocket and retrieved his cell phone.

You've been acting funny lately. Every time I try to see you, somehow you're busy. I don't like that.

Stop acting like a two-year-old. I told you last week I had plans with Ava.

Well I had something special planned for us, but I get it. Do the husband thing, but I want you to get this. After the speech Sunday, my private jet will be fueled up and we are getting away for the evening, so tell Mrs. Ashford something, but don't mess this up. It's important to me and I will not accept no for an answer.

Okay.

'Same old Walter,' Grant thought. *'Always insisting things go his way.'*

Grant had his hands full with him, and even though he liked Walter a lot, the man was a little too bossy for his liking. Grant was used to being the aggressor in his relationships, not the bitch. After Michael Addison, he had made a conscious effort to be the dominant person. That way, when and if he chose to bail, he could do so with no worries. He'd started to walk away from Walter right after their first encounter. He'd had a bad feeling he was getting into something that was a little deeper than he wanted to be involved in, and at times, he hated that he hadn't followed his first mind for the second time in his life.

The whole secret group of powerful men who were intertwined in the city of Detroit was almost like an underground cult of some sort, but now it was too late for Grant to back out. The group consisted of judges, lawyers, doctors, police officials, educators, and movers and shakers in the automotive industry. He understood, that if he did walk away, he would be destroyed or even killed for fear of him leaking information. His career and his marriage would be ruined, taking his mental state down with it. His relationship with his son would most likely be jeopardized as well and that relationship was more important to him than anything in the world.

He knew when Jalen had gone to prison that it was most likely Walter's doing. It had taken some time for him to muster up the courage to investigate, but he'd figured it out and that was why he couldn't wait to show Walter the evidence he'd discovered. However, he had to be strategic when dealing with Walter. Grant didn't want Walter to sabotage his plans to free Jalen, so he'd forged Walter's name on the exoneration papers and wanted to wait until Jalen was free before he told him what he had done. He hoped he wouldn't be extremely angry, but Walter was a master at disguising his emotions and Grant would probably never know how he really felt. For now, he just wanted to reveal what he'd discovered and not tell him about Jalen's release. Grant figured he could get a read on him if he paid close attention.

In the beginning, his conscience had told him Walter was the one, but he had hoped in his heart that it wasn't true. Who would frame an innocent man? At times, Grant wondered if he'd gotten in over his head by dealing with Walter, and he also had a feeling Walter had done some snooping into his past and that Michael Addison hadn't become the Lions' coach by luck or coincidence. It was just too much luck and too big of a coincidence.

If he hadn't learned anything else from his wife, he'd learned the art of manipulation and how it actually worked. He knew wholeheartedly he had to take a play out of her handbook again if he were to ever be happy. "How?" was the question he asked himself everyday as he walked through their marble foyer on his way to work. "How can I find true happiness? Hopefully," he prayed, "no one else will have to get hurt behind it."

"Honey, I'm ready. Are you okay?" she asked, looking at the distraught look on her husband's face as he stood in the kitchen.

"Yes, of course," Grant replied, telling a lie. "I was just thinking about my speech this coming Sunday."

"Grant Ashford, will you stop worrying about something you already know how to do? You have given a million-and-one speeches and everyone I've witnessed has garnered you a standing ovation, so what do you think is going to be different now?"

"You're right, baby. I just don't want to tense up in front of the camera. Millions of people who don't even have anything to do with the city will be tuning in and watching. This was a bold move, but I guess a good one," he said, giving a half-wry, half-fake smile.

"Let momma kiss them juicy lips. That should make it better. Now come on, let's go; I'm hungry," Ava said, walking over to Grant and kissing him lovingly and softly on his lips. She gently wiped her lipstick from his mouth and he assisted her with putting on her cape.

"Oh yeah, I almost forgot to tell you something, honey. After the speech on Sunday, I have to fly to Washington with Walter for a Monday morning meeting," he said as he spun her around and kissed her on the forehead.

Then they finally left for dinner.

Chapter 4

Grant pulled the Mercedes up to the restaurant where the valet worker in his red crushed-velvet vest was waiting to park the next vehicle. Ava loved to dine at Ruth's Chris Steakhouse at least once a month, so Grant made sure it was something they did. He always went above and beyond to keep her happy, thinking it would keep her mentally preoccupied and not allow her womanly intuition to kick in regarding his extracurricular activities.

"Hello, Mr. Councilman," the valet greeted Grant, recognizing him. Grant nodded. "We will put you right up front next to Mr. Billy Mundane."

He opened Ava's door and held it for her, greeting her as well. She smiled, because one thing she really enjoyed was being Mrs. Grant Ashford.

That was another thing about the city of Detroit: Since all the big-time businesses like Motown had left, the biggest stars and most-talked-about people were the Detroit athletes, judges, local business owners, and local politicians. They were celebrities now and a part of the upper echelon of people who attempted to keep the economy flowing. They were often referred to as The Elites. It was nothing to visit a local nightclub and see a popular politician or a Detroit Pistons' or Lions' player out mingling with regular civilians.

Grant wasn't any different than any of the others, because he did his share of civilian mingling. During his first term, he had been a tad bit more reserved and laid back, but during his second term, he'd made a conscious effort to network and be seen at local restaurants, concerts, and neighborhood businesses. He'd made it a point to loosen up and give people the chance to get to know him outside of the office.

He was still private to a certain extent and not like some of the other politicians; with Grant, there had never been any dirt that had surfaced to tarnish the Ashford name. As far as the city knew, he was a happily-married man with a smart son and a promising career, which could one day place him in the White House. "Clean-cut Grant" was what some called him; some people had gone so far as to nickname him "The Motor city Messiah". The one he liked the best was a moniker coined by a writer from the Detroit News, "The Inner-city Savior". He figured the reporters who wrote those articles were receiving some type of backend money from Walter.

He knew, even though most citizens thought he was the best thing since sliced bread, some people had the belief that no one involved in politics was that clean. An overly-zealous and retired investigative local news anchor named Clyde Byrd had it in for Grant. He had a podcast called *A Little Byrdie Told Me,* where he spilled the tea on the movers and shakers in Detroit. Clyde currently worked for the *Michigan Chronicle* newspaper, and he swore, one day, Grant Ashford's dirty laundry would be brought to the light. He'd also said he would be there to get the story.

There was one person who wouldn't be convinced that Grant Ashford wasn't the first angel from heaven, and that was his wife Ava. She believed in him and his passion to change the world, one city block at a time. That had been his campaign slogan when he ran the first time: *Grant Ashford, the man who will change Detroit and the way the city does business, one city block at a time.* His wife had even gone so far as to give away ten thousand free T-shirts with his slogan printed on them. People had been seen all around the city in different-colored T-shirts representing Grant Ashford.

Grant glanced at his wife for a quick second. Ava Ashford was beautiful and still in wonderful shape. When Grant first met the caramel-coated bombshell, he'd known within minutes she was going to be a dangerous temptation. He'd tried to avoid her and respect his inner demons as well, but her long model-like legs and lengthy jet-black hair made her not only desirable but irresistible.

Standing at five-eleven, Ava towered over most of her friends and associates, especially when wearing the heels she loved. When they went out to places like malls and clubs, the men seemed to flock around her, and this made most of her friends feel inferior to her. She also had an aura about her. Most men were mesmerized by her beauty, while others were intimidated by her strong presence. Her four-carat diamond ring also kept the men at bay. Most men didn't want to compete with that.

Ava had heard stories from some of Grant's constituents' wives on how the other men in the cabinet were, but Ava had never openly been worried about her husband. Even when he played in the Saturday poker circle or attended the secret boys' meetings, she didn't sweat it. Grant had always respected her and displayed faithfulness, as far as she was concerned. He did not stay out too late, and the only time he was away from home was when he was on official business. That was okay because she accompanied him on most of his trips, except for the quick one-nighters. Grant would often joke, that as long as it took her to pack, they could have been there and back.

One thing about being a politician's wife, the people loved to see both of them when attending balls, galas, and other events. An inauguration, a bill being passed, or just a baseball being tossed from the pitcher's mound across home plate on opening day was something that showcased good family values, and that made citizens feel more comfortable with their political selection. Grant also felt and believed in the front of his marriage.

"You ready?" Grant asked, extending his arm in a bent fashion. His wife smiled and interlocked her arm with her husband's strong, muscular arm.

"Am I ready? You're the one who must rub egos and elbows with the jet set. I just have to smile and wave," she said, practicing her smile.

That was the same smile that had reeled him in when they'd first met. The same smile she showed the camera when she was accompanying her husband. And the exact same smile she'd showed the doctor when she'd gone behind Grant's back and aborted two children. Grant Ashford wasn't the only one with secrets. Grant knew nothing about Ava's two secret pregnancies or terminations, and that was how she was going to keep it. Ava knew she didn't want any more children but was too vain to take birth control due to a fear of gaining weight. She had already talked him into having a vasectomy, so there was no way to say for sure they were his children.

Telling Grant the truth was not an option. He would never believe she'd done what she'd done to help him and his career. Her reckless transgressions had led to not one but two pregnancies before she'd finally ended the affair. Both times, she'd driven a rental car forty-five minutes north to Toledo, Ohio, to a private doctor whose location was disguised and who specialized in discretion. The small office building had no name on the outside and appointments were scheduled hours apart to prevent patients from seeing each other. Of course, there were additional fees for such solitude, but worth every penny when trying to retain one's privacy.

Ava had managed to pull them both off when Walter had taken Grant to Washington for one of their day trips. She'd made an excuse when he returned that she'd eaten something that upset her stomach for lying in bed the next day. Within forty-eight hours, she was back to her regular self. She hadn't had to worry about him getting suspicious during her healing process; that was actually the least of her worries. For years, even though they were happy, Grant had stopped being the one who initiated sex in their bedroom. At first, she'd thought there was something wrong with her; then, she figured it had to do with him starting to age. Grant would perform like a homerun hitter, literally knocking it out the park, if she requested they make love, but around the time their son Zach turned sixteen, Grant had lost interest in making love. She figured it had to be the stress of being on the city council.

At the restaurant, they were seated at a quiet corner booth, but just as they'd both suspected, the place was crowded with anybody who was somebody. Grant had been deep in thought ever since the valet driver had mentioned Billy Mundane. Grant knew he was the star quarterback for the Detroit Lions, and he wondered, since he was present, if Michael Addison would be there as well. Not wanting to see Michael's face but wanting to at the same time, Grant felt his stomach turn a few times at the memories that kept invading his mind. He didn't want to see Michael, but he knew if it wasn't tonight—which he hoped it wasn't—he would be seeing him in just a few days.

Ava ordered a bottle of wine, asking for the most-expensive bottle, and they both ordered filet mignon, which was what they usually had when they dined there. Grant looked around to see if he saw any familiar faces, specifically Michael's. He didn't see Michael, but he did see Billy Mundane at the bar. Grant felt a small sigh of relief when he saw Billy was accompanied by a young blonde chick who looked to be barely legal. Grant knew he was going to be busy tonight.

He stared at Billy Mundane for a second as he sipped his wine. Not that Billy could ever be a candidate for his bed; just the thought of him in his uniform leading the league in yards thrown was a problem. Grant knew that could have been him in that jersey, playing and leading a team to the best record ever and possibly a super bowl. He'd given it all up, and for what? A piece-of-shit life as a fucking politician. The appearance of their server snapped Grant back to reality.

It didn't take long for their food to be prepared since half the patrons had already eaten. Most were there to drink and share their most-recent conquests or brag about how much money they'd made this week. That is what men did, but in the lifestyles of athletes and politicians, even the women had shit to brag about.

Just as the waiter sat their food in front of them, a familiar scent of cologne entered Grant's nose. He turned and there was Walter, standing behind him with his wife of twenty-two years.

"Honey, what a surprise! Well, look who's here," Walter said, looking deep into Grant's eyes.

Grant didn't remember telling him where he was taking his wife for dinner and was truly pissed about the intrusion.

"Hello, Grant, and hello, Ava. Always a pleasure to see you two!" Walter's wife Nicole exclaimed.

"Look, honey, can you believe this guy?" Walter said, pointing at Grant's plate.

"Look at the size of his steak. Real men don't eat filet mignon. You should have ordered a porterhouse," Walter said, laughing and joking.

Grant was smiling, but he was wondering why Walter hadn't mentioned he had dinner plans also.

"Honey, it's already getting late. Can we sit down and eat?" Nicole asked.

"Why don't we just join the Ashfords? I'm sure they wouldn't mind a little company," Walter said, sliding in the booth next to Grant and pointing for Nicole to join Ava's side.

Grant wanted to object, but it was too late to do any protesting. He hated it when Walter did shit like that. He imposed on him in public every chance he got, and it made Grant feel like a puppet sometimes. He was going to say something to Walter about it, but for now, he had to go with the flow. They talked about the trip to Washington and Ava was actually glad Grant would be gone. That would give her some free time to make a few moves and take care of some business she had been meaning to handle. Walter was going on and on, talking about anything; it was his tactic to keep the women's attention focused on their own conversation.

Grant felt Walter's hand move up his leg as the ladies started another conversation and really weren't paying attention as Walter started talking about a sewer company. Ava was too busy wondering who did Nicole's eyelash extensions and Nicole was trying to see if Ava's perfect white teeth were real or fake. Grant was starting to get an erection, but he knew he couldn't see Walter tonight and a useless boner wasn't good for him. He was sure he didn't want to go home and fuck Ava, but it might end up being his only method of release. He really wished Walter would stop and just have patience, but once Walter attempted to conquer something, he wouldn't quit. Walter fumbled around Grant's crotch until he had finally got his hand inside Grant's zipper.

"Um, excuse me, honey," Grant said, causing Ava to finally look up from her conversation with Nicole. "I need to run to the bathroom really quick."

"Yeah, I think I better go drain my main vein too," Walter said, not wanting to miss this opportunity.

"Walter! Now what kind of language is that to use at the dinner table?" his wife replied.

"Lighten up, baby. We're amongst friends," he said, getting up and heading to the bathroom with Grant following behind him.

Chapter 5

Another Lonely Night...

Vanessa sat on her couch playing with her phone, checking her social media sites to see what was going on in the world. She was really looking for some type of message from her special friend and was very disappointed there wasn't one there. Vanessa was beginning to get tired of the way things had to be for her and her friend. Too much sneaking around wasn't good for the soul, and she was by herself too much at night. Ordinarily, she didn't become attached to people, but this was a little different, something special. She decided to make a quick post on her Facebook page, displaying how she felt, before making herself a nice hot cup of her favorite tea.

She reread it several times, then hit *Post* and walked into her kitchen to fill her tea kettle. While she was running the water into the kettle, she heard her notification go off, meaning someone had clicked *Like* already on her post or left a comment. Vanessa was cautious of who she allowed into her world and she only had a couple hundred Facebook friends, most from her college days and a few family members. She wondered who was on her post already.

After she turned the stove on high, she reached into her robe pocket to retrieve her phone and see for herself. To her surprise, the *Like* she'd received was from her friend she had been missing at that moment, but there was no message accompanying it... just a *Like*. Vanessa smiled and figured her friend must have been tied up doing something important.

She'd never thought in a million years she would be messing around with someone who was married. It was totally against the way she had been raised, but like a lot of people, she'd strayed from the foundation of values of her youth. Her family consisted of church folk who had strong beliefs in their religion and so had she at one time, but she'd fooled herself into believing this wasn't the worst sin of the sins. After all, she wasn't the one who had taken a vow.

Vanessa really wasn't looking to ruin anyone's happy home, but if the home was so happy, why would one party be stepping out? She'd thought about that a lot, and that was what had caused her to snoop a little further into both parties' lives. All Vanessa wanted was happiness for herself and she was willing to play the side-chick for a while to get it. It had had a lot of perks in the beginning and a few more as the relationship progressed.

She cut up a few lemon slices and added them to her mug with an herbal tea bag and some honey to the steaming water. She sipped her hot tea while walking back to her couch to watch television before she decided to call it a night. Another miserable and lonely night without a body next to her.

"This is beginning to be for the birds," she said out loud.

Just as she grabbed the remote, her phone went off again, giving her another notification. This time it wasn't a social media notification, but one from her regular text messages. It was close to midnight and she wondered who would be texting her at this hour.

Sorry I couldn't see you tonight. I read your post as you probably already know. I really wanted to stop by your place. We went out to dinner tonight and we're still here. The restaurant kept it open for us. The place is swarming with politicians, almost feels like the campaign office at the restaurant. Actually, I would rather be in your arms. Don't worry though. Our day is coming.

Vanessa smiled when she read the text. She'd just remembered seeing something about a dinner arrangement on her computer. She felt like, even though her friend had sent a text message, it still wasn't enough. It was thoughtful and all, but she needed a release and one only her special friend could make occur.

> *It's cool. I'm home chilling, drinking some hot tea, wishing you were here. Guess I will re-watch my favorite movie* Stay in Your Place *again. You have a good night and I know we can make it up to each other in a couple of days... Love you...*

She figured the "love you" sentiment was a nice added touch and one to make her friend feel a little something inside when they read it. Vanessa had said she loved her friend, but she wasn't sure if she was in love. How could she be so stupid as to fall in love with someone who had taken a vow with someone else before God? One that ended with, *'til death do us part*?

She crossed her legs on her couch and continued sipping her tea, thinking about how long she would stay in the situation she was in. Not that she actually wanted her lover to leave the marriage either; that was not what she was contemplating. She knew, even if they did separate, a new situation would come with trust issues because of the way they'd gotten together. That never failed, and Vanessa, being a realist, didn't understand why folks didn't believe that. What makes a person cheat with a person, then think the cheater is going to reform and remain faithful to them once they are together? In Vanessa's mind, most cheaters were bored people. They could have the best situation in the world but still step outside it for a thrill that could cost them everything.

One good thing she figured was she only had about a year or two left to be in Detroit, so maybe it was just something for her to do while she finished this term up with her boss. She wasn't going to stick around and be an employee when he won the mayoral seat; that just wasn't going to be the highlight of her life, the mayor's personal assistant. It didn't even have a Vanessa Jones' ring to it.

But Vanessa felt, if she was going to play games, she might as well play on the level she was playing. People in high places did whatever was necessary to keep their name and personal business hidden from the media. At least that was what she was banking on. It was going to cost a pretty little penny to go to law school and start her own private law firm in New York, and she had an idea where the money was going to come from. The Big Apple was her final destination, she figured, an office on the top floor of a high-rise with a corner view overlooking the busy downtown streets.

That was part of her decision to play her cards right with her friends. She had been dealt a good hand already and she knew her only move was to play it the way it was given to her. She felt she had come too far to fold the winning hand she had been dealt, so her plan was to force her opponents to fold. Vanessa was well aware that what she was doing was wrong, but she had come too far to think about folding her own hand and she wasn't going to turn back.

For the last six months, Vanessa had been compiling bits and pieces of information which hadn't made sense at first. It all had started to come together when a carrier dropped off a confidential envelope from a private investigator for her boss and she'd opened it to view the contents. Usually that was procedure anyway, to open Grant's mail, but not when it was marked *Confidential.* Vanessa hadn't realized it said confidential until after she'd opened it. The contents were something she was sure he didn't want her to see.

Apparently, there were some corrupt things going on within the police department, and surely, someone would be willing to pay for this secret. Life was a dirty game, she'd thought as she looked at the contents of the envelope that day. Anyone else would have thought, oh my goodness, and been unsure of how to handle holding this information, but it only had fueled her greed and her goal to obtain her happiness by becoming successful.

Vanessa made copies of what was inside, obtained a new envelope, marked it *Confidential*, and called another carrier service to have them pick up the envelope, just to redeliver it at four p.m. when she knew her boss would be back from his meetings. The delivery man's timing was perfect. He walked into the office just as Grant was coming through the door. She'd signed for it and placed it directly in his hand.

Vanessa walked into her bedroom and sat on her bed, thinking about her life and what was to become of it. She then reached over into her nightstand drawer and took out an envelope that contained emails, pictures, and letters that had come from someone in prison. Vanessa scanned them and uploaded them to her Cloud, but never in a million years would she have guessed the city councilman, who was married to a beautiful woman, was on the down low.

To Vanessa, down-low men were just low-down, dirty dogs. She had nothing against gay men, but she loathed gay men who misled women and lived double lives. That's a very despicable act. A woman should at least have the choice to decide if she wanted to be in a relationship with a man who had sex with other men. How can a man believe it's okay for his wife not to know his true sexual preference?

Vanessa's father was a down-low man who'd decided to up and leave Vanessa's mother when she was thirteen years old to go be "free" to love who he wanted to love—meanwhile, leaving three children behind. Vanessa had dated many men and become promiscuous at a young age searching for her father's love. In college, she began to experiment with women. Vanessa loved who she wanted to love, but she was honest and gave people the option her father had neglected to give her mother.

All this time, she had been trying to push up on Grant Ashford, in hopes of furthering her career in politics for the experience, but he had avoided her attempts for other reasons. At first, Vanessa thought she'd lost her edge and was thinking maybe she had loss her sex appeal.

Maybe she didn't have it together like she thought or maybe she wasn't pretty enough, but she'd quickly realized that wasn't it at all. She had a vagina and *that* was the real problem. Grant Ashford wasn't interested in it or her, and obviously his marriage was a front.

The good thing was Grant was totally clueless about the information Vanessa knew about him. She'd kept all the letters from the guy named Jalen Ross, who was in jail. Jalen had said some pretty incriminating shit in the letters he was hoping only the councilman would read. Some of the descriptions he'd given about their encounters had even made her pussy wet reading them. The sad thing about it was she could tell this man was still in love with Grant. He sounded like he was ready to come out the closet and let the world know it too. Vanessa wondered if that was what had gotten him in trouble. Maybe things were getting too heavy and that was why someone had set him up.

She wondered if her boss had had something to do with the man going to prison, to hide and keep his secret life hidden. She knew people would go to extremes to certain people, their reputations, their money, but most importantly, incriminating details they wanted to keep secret. Vanessa knew a lot of secrets and information from sneaking and reading private emails of others, and hopefully, soon, she would be well-compensated for her knowledge.

The man had received a sentence of ten years in prison and five years' probation, but somehow, he'd managed to get exonerated and have his charges vacated. The heartbroken lovebird would be coming home soon. That was part of the information in the envelope the carrier had delivered to the office that day. When she'd opened it, there were two signed affidavits supporting the release of the prisoner Jalen Ross.

What really had her mind boggled was one of the affidavits had been signed by the governor himself. That seemed very peculiar to her because she'd assumed Walter and Grant may have been involved too. There had always been rumors about Walter and the things you had to do to receive his favors. He and Grant were pretty close, but why would Walter Burke help out a man who was the ex of his current lover?

Vanessa felt in her heart something was wrong, a deep feeling of trouble piercing her soul about the city's soon-to-be mayor. She didn't know if it was a woman's intuition or just a gut feeling, but she wholeheartedly believed there had to be more to the story. Her criminal justice degree, coupled with numerous hours of watching *The First 48* and *Law & Order,* told her there was something more to this "evidence", and yet, she still hadn't pinpointed why the governor would want to help this man out.

"Olivia Benson, eat your heart out," she said out loud and chuckled to herself. Benson was her favorite character on *Law & Order*, and Vanessa knew she would agree there was something wrong with this case. Vanessa had enough evidence to bring down the whole cabinet of Detroit political appointees, but that wasn't her business. If the city voters voted to have down-low brothers in office, that was their issue to deal with.

She wasn't even sure, when everything was said and done, how long she was going to stay in Detroit, but she knew it wouldn't be much longer, because she was planning to leave as soon as she got paid—which would be sooner than later. She wanted that corner view in New York, but Texas was slowly becoming the new Georgia, with tons of people migrating there for opportunity and the promise of a good future. Vanessa was all over the place in her mind with her grandiose plans to relocate. Detroit winters were too cold for her. Why not be somewhere where she could be cute all year around? Maybe California or even Florida. Somewhere, anywhere was going to be better than Detroit. One thing for sure, she couldn't remain in the city after extorting the people on her list.

She smiled as she thought about relocating and all the money she would have to obtain her law degree and start her law firm once she got there. When the time was right, these people were going to pay nicely to keep their secrets safe, especially Grant and Walter.

"Yes, baby, nothing like having the right info on the right people," she said out loud.

She chuckled as she put her collected documents back in the envelope for safekeeping and put them back in her nightstand. She made a mental note to upload her latest piece of information to her cloud in the morning. Vanessa wrapped her body in her heated blanket and called it a night, smiling as she drifted off to sleep.

Chapter 6

Sunday Morning, October 2nd...

The cell bars broke and it was that time. Jalen Ross hadn't expected to be leaving prison until Monday, but since there was no Monday transport heading to Detroit, the warden had okayed a twenty-four-hour early release rather than make him wait an extra day. He figured saving the extra money and the manpower to deliver just one inmate all the way from Jackson to downtown Detroit was worth it, especially since he had three inmates leaving that night who were being transferred for Monday morning court appearances.

Jalen wasn't arguing one bit. A day early meant he couldn't possibly live up to the old cliché his father used to say when he was a kid: *A day late and a dollar short.* He was going to be a day early, so he couldn't be a dollar short, and on top of that, he couldn't wait to get out of his damn cell and away from his hating-ass cellmate, who swore up and down Jody was sexing his wife every night. That was just the hater in him, because he was never getting out to get between another woman's legs.

Jalen still didn't know much about Jody and who the fuck he was even talking about, but he was sure if a Jody did exist, it would be one of them fake-ass Christian brothers from the church. Her father kept other men in his wife's presence, so Jalen was sure the pastor was most likely trying to fix his baby girl up with someone else, someone who was on that church shit. That wasn't him, and he'd told her that from day one. It wasn't like he'd led her on. He actually had told her he wasn't into church the day he'd met her in the grocery store.

He knew upon meeting her, by the way she was dressed and the first words that came out her mouth, that she was a Bible pusher. He'd tried giving church a chance, but when it didn't work, he didn't think they would go very far in their relationship. There was something about Taylor though, something innocent and sweet, that drove him crazy. It might had been the fact that she was playing hard to get in the bed. She would scream that mess about she was saving her goodies for her husband.

Jalen had thought dating her was a waste of time, but every time she came by his apartment, she would either have a gift or a plate of warm food. They would sit and watch movies and talk, and sometimes kiss until he got blue balls. He wanted to fuck her badly, almost to the point where he was about to give in and join the church. They were spending so much time together that she suggested he move in with her.

The night prior to them moving in together, Taylor offered to stop by with dinner and help Jalen pack. He purposely brought home a couple bottles of wine and a sex pill the clerk at the corner store claimed increased a woman's libido. Jalen didn't know how true it was since he'd tried some over-the-counter packets that were supposed to work wonders for a man and they hadn't, but it was worth a try.

That night, he'd crushed three of them up and put them in her glass of lemonade. She had prepared tacos and Spanish rice. After eating, they'd decided to watch a film on a Christian movie network. He watched her drink two glasses of lemonade. After the movie ended, she picked up her coat and he'd known the pills were bullshit. They started kissing at the door and she'd started unzipping his jeans. One thing led to another and they'd spent two days in his bed, only getting up to shower and eat.

Taylor admitted to not being a virgin, but she didn't have to with the way she'd performed. It had felt like he was in bed with a Christian porn star, because she prayed every time she came.

That was some weird shit to him, but it also had turned him on.

"YES, LORD! YES!" she would scream.

At first, he would get mad. *'Here I was, putting in all the work, and she's calling His name? How disrespectful was that?'* Jalen thought and laughed to himself as the bus came to a halt.

The guards in the front of the transport bus exited the vehicle, and started getting their keys as well as their weapons ready to move everyone on the bus. Jalen was the only one of the four inmates on the bus who was going home. He knew he wasn't going to say anything about it to any of the other riders. It was said that people who weren't going home despised people who were, and he didn't plan on finding out if that rumor was true. Two of the men were returning to court for stage one of their appeal process, and the other one was facing more charges he hadn't been sentenced for yet. So, between getting denied and getting more time, he rode in silence, thinking about his life. After an hour of riding and reflecting, Jalen had arrived at his destination.

"Okay, boys, here we are, the old Wayne County Jail," the fat white guard said.

The jail was on Clinton Street and Jalen hadn't called Taylor to let her know he would be arriving home a day early. He figured he would surprise her and pop up at the crib. What he hadn't taken into consideration was how long the release paperwork was going to take and that she would be gone to church by the time the process was complete. He was escorted off the bus and into a holding cell. It took about four hours before a deputy came to see him and get him set up to be released.

None of the clothes he'd had on when he originally went to prison fit him anymore. His jeans, his shirt, not even his boxers fit. Everything was now two sizes too small. The only thing he could wear from his intake bag was his sneakers. He hadn't realized he had gained so much weight, but he was happy because it was all muscle. At that moment, he felt like the new-and-improved, buffed-up Jalen, and he couldn't wait to get back to his old lifestyle and see some of his old friends. He also had a special friend who was on his mind. His special friend was the only one besides Taylor who'd kept up with him while he was gone.

That meant a lot to Jalen, but his mind kept veering off, giving one other person a lot of thought—Grant Ashford, the Detroit councilman who didn't give a fuck about him obviously. Jalen had his work cut out for him now that he was back on the streets. He was free, but he still wanted to know who had set him up and why. One thing was for sure, he was going to use his special friend to help him find out.

He pushed open the doors to the Wayne County Jail still wearing his prison clothes, but he didn't care. He was so happy to be free that he almost bent down to kiss the ground when he walked outside. They'd given him one phone call, but instead of calling Taylor, he'd called his special friend, who was on duty at that moment. He started to pitch-a-bitch because he was ready to get away from jail and fast; plus, he was starving and wanted some real food. But he was just happy to be free. His friend couldn't make it, so he'd sent an Uber to pick him up. Jalen was okay with that because he knew he would be seeing him and he knew it would be soon.

He noticed a check cashing store on the corner, so he walked down the street to cash the $497 check he'd received for the money on his books. After entering the store, he realized he didn't have a driver's license to cash the check and turned to exit the store.

The Arab man behind the glass yelled, "WHAT'S THE MATTER, FRIEND?" just as Jalen reached the door.

Jalen informed him that he didn't have an ID to cash his check and the man asked if had his prison ID, which he did. The store charged twenty percent as a check-cashing fee and Jalen thought that was ridiculous, but he realized he didn't have many options.

The man behind the glass was a good salesman. Ten minutes later, Jalen was walking out the door wearing a new jogging suit, with two hundred dollars in cash, a new cellphone, and a slice of pizza, just in time to catch his ride.

Chapter 7

The Detroit Lions were in the lead by a field goal going into halftime. Ford Field had been sold out, and it was only the second time the attendance had been this high at a Lions' game since the greatest running back of all time Barry Sanders had retired. The crowd was going crazy as Tab Rasul, a popular Detroit singer, took to centerfield and performed two of her latest hits.

The announcer then introduced the guest speaker, Grant Ashford, who walked onto the stage accompanied by his wife Ava, his son Zach, and his secretary Vanessa Jones. Grant stood center stage and waved and smiled to the people as he watched the big screen in the front of him to make sure his makeup was intact. He hadn't wanted to wear makeup because he felt it was for women; but even though he was insecure with his masculinity, he wasn't going to allow the world to know that little secret about him.

Grant looked around, continuing to wave and smile at the people like he was an old pro at it. The people of Detroit were going crazy; it was like he had already won the election. Once the crowd finally quieted down, he started in with his speech, first cracking a joke to get them warmed up.

Vanessa smiled as Grant went into his delivery of the speech she'd helped him prepare. She had spent an hour this morning going over the speech again when he'd emailed her his final draft. It was good but still needed a woman's touch, and she was the perfect person for the job. Grant looked up while speaking, noticing there was a blimp circling the stadium with the words running in bright lights, "Grant Ashford for Mayor". As much as he hadn't wanted the position at first, he now felt like he deserved it and he could serve his city well. The fans were quiet as he was about to deliver his finishing lines.

"And with all I have promised you here today, you have my word that Grant Ashford will make a change, by any means necessary," he said, completing his speech with a little help from the words of the late-great Malcolm X.

He heard chants of, "T-shirts! T-shirts! T-shirts!", and knew the people wanted more T-shirts. Before he walked off the stage, he made sure to put that job in Ava's hand. She was excellent at the little things, as long as it consisted of shopping and spending money. Ava waved to the crowd as they all saw her beautiful face on the big screen and went ballistic knowing, that once again, the inner city would be walking around in Grant Ashford shirts. She was a good first lady in the eyes of many. Vanessa just smiled, as the Ashfords were becoming more popular than ever.

"Hey, Pop, we don't get Secret Service yet?" Zach asked playfully.

Zachery Ashford was standing alongside Vanessa and he found it hard as hell to keep his eyes off her legs. She was in her mid-twenties and not that much older than him, so he figured, when the time was right, he might as well shoot his shot. He was in medical school and planned on becoming a doctor, in addition to possibly being the son of Detroit's next mayor. That alone should make him a good catch for any woman who was on the market.

"I don't think it's in the budget, Son," Grant said jokingly.

He couldn't believe the instant change of heart he'd just had. He was all in and wanted the position as mayor, and now he wasn't going to turn back. The universe must have had it written for his life to go the way it was going. He had a quick thought about Walter and knew it would be a great night tonight when they celebrated.

As security escorted them off the stage, the pain in Grant's ass, reporter Clyde Byrd, was standing by the team, trying to shove his microphone into Grant's face.

"SO, IS THAT HOW YOU PLAN ON WINNING THE ELECTION, COUNCILMAN ASHFORD, BY BRIBING THE CITIZENS OF DETROIT FOR YOUR VOTE WITH FREE T-SHIRTS?" Clyde yelled toward Grant, who ignored him. Grant didn't feel this nuisance was worth his attention.

Grant and his family continued to walk toward the Lions, and it was the first time since Michael's arrival in Detroit that the two of them had come face-to-face. Neither of them knew who'd come up with the bright idea that Grant should shake hands with the whole team, but Grant imagined it was Walter's, if no one else's. Walter was brilliant at running a campaign and a genius at putting the people he wanted in office.

Zach bumped into his father by mistake as they were departing in a single-file line. Grant didn't realize how long he had been standing there holding Michael's hand. It was too long as their eyes locked and his suppressed memories raced to the forefront of his mind. Michael had been the first man Grant had actually had sex with. He'd messed around in high school with a few friends, but they'd never gotten serious. He was a virgin when he and Michael had made love. Michael was so passionate, yet so gentle, loving, and tender with him; it was the best night of his life, even to this day.

"Great job so far with the team," Grant said and finally moved along.

When he got to Billy Mundane, who was Michael's new love, the handshake was very quick and Billy Mundane looked like he didn't have any words for the mayoral candidate. Billy had noticed the look on both Grant and Michael's faces when they'd shaken hands and sensed this wasn't their first meeting. A tinge of jealousy invaded Billy's spirit and he felt betrayed by Michael. In fact, he felt a little heartbroken and decided he would pay him back on the field in the second half of the game.

Grant felt the apprehension in the team's star quarterback and keep it moving right on down the line. He was really ready to go so he could do some paperwork and prepare to leave tonight with Walter, but he did look Billy Mundane in the eyes and he saw something there. Grant didn't want to speculate, but another memory surfaced about Michael. It made Grant think that he too was once a Billy Mundane. Actually, they sort of looked alike when Grant was his age, and both carried similar stats as quarterbacks. Maybe it was Michael's thing; his star quarterbacks must turn him on. Whatever Grant may have thought, it wasn't his business anymore what Michael Addison did or who he did it with. That chapter of his life was closed and that was how he needed it to stay.

Grant didn't know Michael had been making an effort to stay away from him, and Michael didn't know Grant knew he was there and also making the same conscious effort to steer clear of him. For the both of them, it could mean nothing but danger. Grant knew it and Michael did as well. Grant knew he hadn't given Michael true closure and that was because he truly hadn't had a reason to break it off. Yes, Ava had been carrying his baby at the time, and yes, he was about to become a father, but none of that was the real reason.

The real reason was because he had been falling deeply in love with Michael and he was afraid of love. Afraid because of how it made him feel and afraid because he hadn't truly loved himself until he'd met Michael. Giving love and receiving love, combined with a newfound self-love, was way too much for Grant to handle. He was afraid and outside of his comfort zone. Life with Ava would be easier.

Finally, they made it to the limo and all gathered inside. Grant instructed the driver to drop his son and wife off at their home since their home was the closest. Vanessa was next. Then to the office for him to finish some business he had started. When they were alone in the car, Vanessa went to acting the way she frequently did when she and Grant were alone. She was sitting across from Grant in the rear of the extended Suburban limousine the taxpayers had paid for, her skirt hiked up, her shoes off, and her legs spread slightly apart as they talked. Grant had to exert great discipline not to look downward. It was clear from his peripheral vision that she wasn't wearing any panties and he knew she was very well aware of what she was doing.

"I think the speech was awesome," she said, shifting a little sideways, giving more of a view.

She didn't know if she was just wanted to tease him or if she really wanted her boss to take her into her apartment and fuck her. She knew she would be seeing his wife Ava tonight and they would party. She'd also had a few visions about their son Zach. He looked like he could give a good work out in the bedroom.

"Yes. Thanks to you and your creative abilities, I must say it went very well," Grant replied. He noticed they were about a block from her home and took the chance to steal a quick peek.

"Up here on the right," he called out through the privacy glass to the driver.

Vanessa gathered her iPad and purse, and put her shoes on as she prepared to exit the vehicle. Her mission was complete; she was now one hundred percent sure about her boss. No man in his right mind would have passed up an open opportunity to have sex with her right now at this moment. She had done everything to Grant, except say, "Come fuck me." She knew now, that even if she had said that, Grant Ashford was not interested in her in that way.

She stood, half bent over, kissed her boss on the cheek, wished him a safe flight, and climbed out the truck.

Chapter 8

Second Half...

Both sports announcers were livid. They were losing their minds at how Billy Mundane was playing during the second half of the game. One announcer said it was going to go down as one of the worst losses in Lions' history, while the other one claimed Billy Mundane must have caught an allergic reaction to something during halftime.

It was now fourth quarter and the Lions, who'd once led by three, trailed by twenty-one. The teams' defense had done all they could to try to control their opponent's offense, but every time they got the ball back for the Lions, Billy Mundane threw another interception. By the middle of the fourth, the defense was worn out. They had spent entirely too much time on the field and couldn't sustain it any longer.

The locker room was quiet during showers. Billy Mundane sat in front of his locker, again being the last one to get cleaned up and dressed out. The players started dispersing to their fancy cars to head to their even-fancier homes. Most of them didn't trip on the loss because it didn't hurt the standings, but there were a few mumbles from some of the players referring to the playoffs, which were right around the corner.

Billy didn't say anything to anybody because he was the star and he felt he didn't owe any of them an explanation for having one bad game. He also felt like he'd carried the load this far and one loss wasn't as bad as the teams' record last year before he'd arrived. At this point in the season last year, the Lions had only taken to the field because it was mandatory for a team to finish out its remaining schedule. They'd had only one win and couldn't do anything but wait for a draft pick. A couple of the remaining players who had finished dressing walked past Billy and patted him on the shoulder.

"There's always next week, kid," one said.

"Good game. We got this," his tight end said, heading out to his Lamborghini.

Finally, they were all gone, and Billy got ready for his shower. He took a quick one and stood back in front of his locker drying off. A few seconds after removing the towel from his waist, he delivered a fast right hook dead into his locker.

"Careful; we need that wrist next week," a voice said behind him.

"You don't give a fuck! You think I didn't see that shit out there?" Billy responded to Coach Addison.

The coach wasn't crazy, so he knew what shit Billy was talking about, but he was going to play it off—if he could.

"You mean their defense? They weren't all that. The tapes told us exactly what plays they would run when they were behind," Coach replied, being condescending.

"Don't try to fuck with my head, Michael! You know I'm not talking about no damn defense and them being behind. I'm talking about the person you are fucking and doing only God knows what else with behind my back."

"Whoa, slow down, baby. You're going a little too fast."

"Am I? If I'm going too fast, why did I just do a search on Google and find out you'd coached Grant Ashford in college, and he was a star quarterback? Damn, at least he could have been a kicker or a running back. You must have a thing for the quarterbacks, huh, Coach?"

There was an awkward pause from the coach. He hadn't figured Billy would go a step further and research either of their pasts. The coach shook his head mutely for a second, thinking how to respond. He knew Billy was right and on to him about Grant. He looked at Billy with anger, anxiety and excitement warring in the pit of his stomach, not sure what to think, let alone what to say.

"Listen, Billy," he said, walking up behind him while he was still naked.

He was going to give it his best shot to try to salvage whatever relationship they had, but he also knew seeing Grant today, actually touching him again, had brought back a flood of feelings he'd thought were gone. But they hadn't vanished; they'd only been covered up as he'd gone on with his life. Billy was the only man he'd ever loved after Grant. He had messed with every quarterback he'd coached between Grant hurting him and Billy loving him, but those had all been flings, nothing serious—until Billy.

"You're correct. I did coach Grant Ashford, but that was many moons ago. And, to be honest with you, we did have a little something, but nothing compared to what you and I share," Michael said, touching Billy on his lower back. "I'm a football coach and that is what I'm good at. I can't untangle all the threads of my life; I wish it was that easy," Coach said.

"Did you love him?" Billy asked, looking over his left shoulder, his face expressionless as he waited for Michael Addison to answer his question.

When Michael looked at Billy, the locker room lights revealed hurt and sadness. He could sense concern brewing under the surface of Billy's brown eyes. Michael had to be careful not to say anything to hurt Billy. Now wasn't the time to ruin the team's whole season.

"Do you really want to know the answer to that question?" Michael asked a question of his own as he turned that mocking, cynical gaze on Billy.

Billy wasn't quite sure now if he wanted to know, but when he'd looked at Michael when he asked him if he wanted to know, the tight line that curled his bottom lip was a sure sign it was more painful than pleasurable, with the pain points going to him and the pleasure points in favor of Grant. Yet, he was only human and he did want to know the truth. It wasn't like it would leave the shower room and become public.

"No," Michael said, then added rather nonchalantly, "I had a different agenda back then. I'm not sure I knew how to love anyone in those days, not even myself. I was unsure of me and what my future was supposed to hold. Billy, you know we cannot turn back the hands of time and change the things we regret doing. If I could, I would move both hands on the clock backward. But even though a lot of things I may have done have come with some regrets, I feel like it was all part of a course that was out of my control, and a part of what got me here today, standing next to you."

He'd lied as good as he could and hoped it worked. The tension in the room was thinning out as the room filled with intimacy. Billy was standing there naked when his manhood started to show it was ready for some attention. Michael's response was perfect in Billy's opinion. Michael's opening up and being honest with him—at least so he'd thought—was a turn on.

Michael's reply was all Billy needed to hear to make him feel like he was still number one in Michael's life. All his life he had been rejected, and not so much by other people, but by himself—scared of what people would think of him and how differently he would be treated. It was cool that the world was now accepting people of his sexuality and pretending they were equal as humans, but he knew it was only surface respect. It didn't matter what laws were passed for people of their community because there would always be people around them who wished for them to burn in hell.

Michael had been a lifesaver for Billy Mundane. He had treated him the way he'd wanted to be treated, which was tender, but rough when needed. To Billy, their relationship was all that mattered in the big world of cruel people. He felt more than just that plain old kiss-me, hug-me love for Michael. He felt he was in a safe space, with an unconditional state of love for this man.

He'd wanted to give Michael a perfect record and win every game of the season. The world would see him as the greatest coach ever, even surpassing his own idol, Vince Lombardi. Billy wanted to give him the world on a silver platter. He had a notion the two of them would live a long, happy life together after the world of football was long gone from their lives.

"I'm sorry, Michael," Billy said as he turned to face Michael and reached for his zipper.

Michael didn't know why he was apologizing. "For what, baby? What are you sorry for? I was wrong and should have told you about Grant when I knew he was coming to do a speech here; at least I could have given you that much respect. I'm the one who should be apologizing."

"No; I blew the game on purpose," Billy said, finally freeing Michael's manhood from his pants and dropping to his knees.

Michael ran his right hand over the tricked-out braids lining the top of Billy's head. "There's always next week, baby," he said, closing his eyes and enjoying the sexual bliss Billy was bestowing upon him.

Chapter 9

Vanessa entered her apartment, smiling and extremely soaking wet between her legs. She had been so wet that, even if she did wear panties, they would need to go straight into the washing machine. Vanessa was feeling some type of way from teasing Grant and she knew she had to do something to cure the horny feeling engulfing the insides of her vaginal walls. She knew after midnight that she would be hooking up with Ava, who could eat pussy like a porn star. The last time the two of them had gotten together, Ava had given her the nickname of Ms. Waterfalls, because every three minutes, she was gushing a glacier of her juices all over Ava's face and Ava didn't mind one bit.

She undressed, removing her blouse, bra, and tight-fitting skirt, standing in front of the mirror. She fondled her breasts, raising them one at a time and kissing as close to the nipple as she could. She then looked in the mirror at her gorgeous shape and smiled again, knowing the only reason her boss Grant Ashford was not carrying her in the house and sticking it to her was because he must like men more than he liked women.

She chuckled at her thoughts, then went to her desk and powered up her MacBook to look up something. Still naked and wet, she fingered herself as she waited for the search engine screen to pop up. She moaned with pleasure, taking her fingers out one-by-one and tasting them.

Finally, her computer was ready to do some due diligence and help her look up a few things. The first thing she looked up was the Circuit Court records. There she found the case against the man named Jalen Ross who recently had been exonerated. It didn't say much, but some new evidence had been introduced by a high-ranking government official that proved Jalen had been wrongfully convicted. From the other paperwork, Vanessa had determined the governor as the official, but what still puzzled her was who had actually set up Jalen Ross. That person would be the one willing to pay the most money for her secrecy. It didn't make sense for the governor to send him to jail, then three years later release him, so it must have been Grant, but why?

Vanessa had to put her thinking cap on. Then, it came to her where she had heard that name before. Due to Homeland Security regulations, every call that came into a political office was recorded, just in case a terrorist threat came in. This was when her computer class she'd taken at the University of Michigan was going to come in handy. She opened a private browser and logged into the city's mainframe. There was a slot for the councilman's incoming and outgoing phone calls made from the office. She still didn't have the passkey because that was protected by federal guidelines and only Grant knew the key. The Feds didn't even know his password because they didn't need to know it. Their clearances would allow them to access the system with their own passwords. She'd tried everything from his son's name to his ending stats as a quarterback. Nothing had gotten her in the system.

She had one more bright idea as she picked up the phone to call an old flame of hers who was married and now living in Ohio. The phone rang several times before the voicemail picked up. She was almost ready to give up on her idea until the phone rang back on her end.

"Damn, baby, I was shocked when I saw your name come across my screen," Gary said.

"Surprised? Is that why you didn't answer? Oh, I know. You must be busy with your little wife," Vanessa responded.

"Still the same old Vanessa, I see; you haven't changed a bit, don't hold back a damn thing. You know something, girl? Your slick mouth was what always turned a brother on about you."

"Ummm mmm, tell me anything. If you were so turned on, I would have been the one wearing that big-ass, three-carat diamond ring and having Tyrese singing at my wedding. So, we know who turned you on and off, don't we?" Vanessa said, touching herself again.

"See, there you go, talking crazy like always. I ain't got long. I'm at the hospital with my wife. She's in labor and about to deliver soon," Gary said, knowing it wasn't a booty call. So what was the purpose of her call?

"GARY! Another one? You knock that damn girl up every year. Anyway, I called you because I need a big favor. I know it's unethical, but I assure you, it's for a good cause."

"I don't know if I like the sound of this, but for your information, Denise miscarried our last child, and after this one, granted God allows it to go right, she is getting fixed. So, we will stop with only three," he explained.

Vanessa felt like an ass for a brief moment. "Aww, I'm sorry to hear that. Well, one thing for sure, you always said you wanted a big family. Now, what I want is to use your federal passcode to get into a phone system at work. I misplaced some information from an important message that was left on our system at work, and I need access to complete an urgent task for my boss. I didn't tell him because I didn't want to appear to be incompetent at my job, I just need to get in and find that message. It contains some very pertinent information and I can't locate it anywhere else. It should only take a minute or two," she lied.

"Unethical is an understatement. Are you asking me to put my career on the line? You're lucky as hell I trust you, and one more thing: You've got to promise me one more shot when we see each other. I saw you on television today and I was like, damn, that ass still looks good!" he said jokingly.

"You got it if you do this for me and promise to wear a rubber. I just might make a special trip to Ohio to let you do your thing. You know we ain't never had an issue in that department," she replied, lying again.

Gary was the worst lay she'd ever had. First of all, he couldn't get it up without taking Viagra. Then, when she was her normal self and got super wet, he'd get so excited, he'd release damn-near on contact. She felt sorry for his wife if he didn't get help for his early-stage erectile dysfunction. She knew she wouldn't have married his limp-dick ass, even if he had given her a six-carat ring and brought Gerald Levert back to sing at their wedding, and the Silky Teddy Bear was her favorite artist of all time.

"Yeah, you've got it, baby," he said, licking his lips and waving to a nurse who was telling him from a distance it was delivery time.

"Look, baby, here's my passcode; use it tonight. I will change it when I get back in the office tomorrow or the next day. They'd have to login if they ever needed to check to see who was in the system. I know it would be hard for me to explain what I was doing in Detroit and logged on, but don't worry about that. I'll just change it first thing tomorrow morning. I'm going to hold you to that promise too," he said, quickly rattling off his passcode and ending the call.

She hung up, glad Gary had found someone to marry his no-sex-drive, limp-dick, bad-head-giving ass. Not only couldn't he fuck, but he couldn't even get down there and make up for it with his tongue. But none of that mattered; she was just glad she had a friend who worked for the federal government and was able to help her.

Vanessa took her last finger out of her own love nest and tasted it, saying out loud, "This is for you, Gary Pearson." She smiled and logged back on to the system. It worked like a charm. She was in and could hear all her boss' phone calls.

Vanessa remembered the last year when Grant had instructed her and was very adamant about his instructions not to accept any calls from a prison. His excuse was the city was experiencing a high volume of calls coming from inmates in the city complaining about the conditions in the jails, and they weren't accepting the calls anymore. He informed her that all complaints must be submitted in writing and that was what she'd told the callers. Grant wasn't aware that his statement was what had inspired Jalen to start writing letters.

As she went up and down the log, surfing the records, the calls showed up. Ten of them were three seconds or shorter, and she knew those were the hang ups she had done when they'd come through and she'd answered, but there were two calls that had lasted a whole fifteen minutes and both calls were back-to-back. Those were the two she listened to.

Just as she'd expected, both calls were from Jalen Ross, the man who was being released. On the first call, they'd mostly talked about his trial and how he had been set up. The second call was when things had gotten heated. She looked at the date and remembered she had been on vacation in Miami on that day because that was her birthday weekend. The temp must have put the calls through to Grant. The conversation between Grant and Jalen had taken a very different turn on the second call.

Jalen was talking about how much he'd missed Grant's touch and Grant seemed to be melting right through the phone. Then Grant appeared to have a change of heart and they began arguing. By the time it was done, Grant had asked Jalen not to ever contact him again. Before Jalen had hung up, he had said the words, "Yeah, we will see if you really mean that."

"DAMN!" she shouted out loud.

Grant was most definitely on the down low, and she knew she had done the right thing by going after the wife instead of putting all her eggs in *his* basket. Her original plan had been to trap him by seducing him and faking a pregnancy, but when she'd befriended Ava, her plans had changed. After Ava revealed the details about their sexless marriage, Vanessa had assumed Grant must be having an affair. His wife was gorgeous and who wouldn't want to have sex with her? So, he must have a side-piece and her plan was to find the other woman.

She overheard him joking with a senator one day about having had a vasectomy. Now that made sense, have one kid to cover up his farce, but Vanessa also had knowledge of Ava's secrets. Ava had confided in her that she'd become pregnant from an affair, which was why she now cheated only with women—no risk of getting pregnant. Ava never said who the man was, but something about their conversation made Ava believe he was still around and close by.

Vanessa was deep in thought, and the ringing of her phone next to her startled her out of her daze. The call was coming in from a private number, and at first, she thought it was Ava, until she looked at her watch. It was still a few hours too early for Ava to be calling her. She knew Grant's flight wasn't scheduled to depart yet. Reluctantly, she answered the call, which she never did for unknown numbers. Ava had an app on her phone that allowed her to change her number and she always called from a 734 area code. The number would never be the same, but the area code would. It was cool because Vanessa had friends who lived in Ann Arbor, Michigan, and since she'd attended University of Michigan, any phone searches wouldn't render anything incriminating.

"Hello," she said into the mouthpiece.

"Hey, beautiful," the caller replied. The voice was male and unfamiliar to her.

"You've obviously got the right person, but who is this?" she laughed.

"Zach, Zach Ashford; we formally met at the speech today."

"Oh, I know who you are. What made you call me?" she asked, fingering herself again. This was about to get interesting and she didn't even have to think this one out.

"I don't know. I'm only in town for a couple more days and I wondered if I could see you. I thought I felt some type of chemistry on the stage between us today."

"Stop lying; you didn't think that. You want to fuck something; I get it. I was once in college too, you know," she replied, eager to give him what he wanted.

If he could get to her in the next thirty minutes, she could screw him, put him out, and clean up for his mother, with neither of them the wiser. It was foolproof and would work. As much as Vanessa liked to taste a little pussy, she still liked her men equally.

"Wait, does that make me a hypocrite?" she thought out loud.

She quickly thought about Gary again and wished he was better at sex, because she would have taken a vacation day to go let him bang her, but he wasn't worth it. Even if he paid for the ticket for her to fly there, it would be like taking a kid to Willie Wonka's chocolate factory and Willie was all out of candy. Her mind was all over the place and she'd forgotten Zach was on the phone.

"Damn, you didn't have to say it like that," Zach replied, snapping her back to the conversation.

"Look, baby boy, you caught me at the right time, but don't tell your parents about this. I love my job, and I think your father will make a great mayor," she said, then gave him her address.

"Your secret is safe with me," he said, ending the call.

Zach was rushing out the Ashford home, moving swiftly. Ava stopped him on his way out the door to ask him where he was going. Her husband had arrived back home, was packing his overnight bag, and was due to leave for his trip. She figured they could drop him off together, and that way, she could come back home, let Zach retire to his room, and be out to see her little boo-thang.

"I have to make a run to see a few old friends," Zach lied as he grabbed the keys to his Porsche.

"You sure that can't wait? Don't you think your father will want to see you before he leaves?"

"Mom, I'm not seven anymore. Besides, Dad is only going to be gone for a day. I'm sure we'll go fishing, play golf, or something before I go back to school."

"Okay, but you know how he gets. Drive safe, and if I'm not here when you get back, there's some roast beef in the fridge if you're hungry."

"I'll be good, Mother," he said, walking out the front door.

He looked at the text his cousin had just sent. Gary had texted him earlier to say he'd seen him onstage standing next to one of his old flings. He mentioned he'd only heard from her when she needed a favor.

Hey man. Vanessa just called me trying to get my passcode to get into your father's call system. Not sure if there is anything to it. I just know you asked me to let you know if anything funny was going on with her.

Zach quickly texted him back:

Please tell me you didn't give it to her!

Gary replied:

Yes I gave it to her. Look, I'm at the hospital with Denise. She just had a healthy baby boy. I didn't have time to go back and forth with Vanessa. You said to let you know and that's what I did. I gotta go, but let me know if you need anything else."

Even though he was pissed, Zach texted his cousin Gary back, thanking him for the information. For a moment, he hoped Vanessa hadn't discovered any of his father's secrets, but then he remembered the plan and it wouldn't have been created if she didn't know anything. Zach wondered if she was just as shocked as he was when he'd discovered his father's secrets.

Three years ago, Zach had found scanned letters and pictures of his dad with men on his father's iCloud. Zach had dropped his iPhone in some water when he was home a few years ago for Christmas break. His dad had given him an old phone he had lying around to use temporarily, but he'd forgotten to log out of the phone. That night, Zac was playing around on the phone and had mistakenly entered Grant's iCloud—where he'd discovered his father, naked with other men in most photos or engaged in sexually-explicit activities with men in the others.

Zach had always wondered where he himself had acquired his desire for men from, and when he had discovered he was just like his father, he'd known. Many say sexuality isn't hereditary, but how did they really know? Zach identified with the lust for a man that Grant had, and he even had a boyfriend back at school. One thing though, he knew a snake when he saw one, and Vanessa Jones was definitely the belly-crawling creature that could make life hard for his father, and at the same time, break up his family. He wasn't going to stand by and allow that to happen.

His first thought had been to use some of his savings to pay her to leave Detroit and not show her face again, but he knew her type and he knew she was after a much bigger prize than the twenty thousand dollars he could offer her. But he wasn't willing to see his father's dreams and aspirations all end because of a snake in their garden. It was time for Zach to become a mongoose and eliminate this potentially-deadly cobra for good.

Chapter 10

Jalen felt like he was a stranger in his own home now that he had finally returned. He'd had sex with Taylor and they had spent most of the early part of the day in bed. He couldn't believe his wife actually had left church to come let him in and had stayed with him. He thought she'd missed him at first, but after a few hours, her energy had changed.

There was something vaguely different about her. She'd talked to him like he wasn't smarter than a fifth grader and he didn't like that. She had stood by him because she'd believed there was no way he could be guilty of child molestation, but maybe now, he was wondering, if she was having second thoughts by the way she was acting.

Jalen even got to wondering about that shit his ex-cellmate had been talking about. Was there a Jody, or a member of the church, who'd gotten in her ear? He noticed she was a little wilder in bed than before he'd left. He tried shrugging off the thought of what another prisoner had said, knowing that people in his position just loved causing other people misery, but maybe there was some truth to his theory.

When she got up and told him she needed to make runs for the church, he'd known if something had changed, that part sure hadn't. How in the hell could she abandon him on his first day back home to do nothing but run and get supplies for her daddy's ministry? That could have waited until tomorrow, he thought as he searched the house for any incriminating clues.

He hadn't found anything as he sat on the new couch watching the halftime show of the game. He scooted up to get closer to the television when Grant Ashford appeared, looking as handsome and debonair as he had the last time they'd been together. It was a crying shame the feeling he had for Grant still existed, when he knew in his heart Grant had moved on and possibly had set him up.

Jalen saw Zach standing beside his father. Zach had really matured in the past few years and looked just like his father; the two of them looked like twins. Jalen still had a lot of resentment pent up inside because of the way Grant had treated him before and while he was locked up. It was like what they'd had never meant a damn thing to Grant. Jalen really had thought they were in love.

He recorded the halftime show and watched it several times over and over, hanging on to every word that came out of Grant's mouth. Even if he wasn't paying attention, just watching his sexy lips move stirred up something deep down inside Jalen.

He turned to a crime show and sunk back into the couch, thinking of that final day in court when the jury had delivered the guilty verdict. Jalen couldn't believe he was heading to prison for a crime he hadn't committed, but when you were set up by someone and they used forensic evidence, you were most definitely going to be found guilty. He had been accused of having sex with a fourteen-year-old girl whom he had never laid eyes on before. The girl, a foster child to a single parent, was being raised by a man named Victor Bennett, who was father by day and prostitute Viola Reeves by night.

Jalen had spent countless hours in his cell wondering why and how Viola had set him up. The two of them had had a real connection. The only thing Jalen could think of was maybe he was upset for the way Jalen had ended things. True, he'd ghosted Victor, but it hadn't been abruptly. They were no longer kicking it how they use to. Jalen had ignored his calls, and finally, he'd stopped calling. But was that serious enough for Victor to set him up to go to prison and be labeled a sex offender for the rest of his life?

They hadn't messed around in months before this had happened. The only times they hadn't used protection was when Victor had given him oral. How in the hell they'd gotten his semen and placed it inside this young girl was still puzzling to him?

Jalen got up and went into the kitchen to make a sandwich and grab a cold beer from the refrigerator when he heard the narrator from the television show talk about a groupie who'd collected an NBA player's semen from a condom he'd used with someone else while she was in his home. She'd entered his bathroom from an adjoining bedroom, retrieved the condom from his trashcan, gone downstairs into his kitchen, and impregnated herself with a turkey baster.

Jalen shook his head in disbelief as he prepared his sandwich, and even said, "Wow!" out loud when the narrator said the woman has receiving ten thousand dollars a month for child support.

The next story was a cold case, where a man had been framed by some very powerful people by switching his DNA. Jalen, who had just reached for his beer, dropped the can and ran back to the television when he heard the commentator.

"Is this a sign? Is this what happened to me?" he asked out loud.

Jalen sat back on the couch and watched the entire story. After it ended, he began to think about the last time he'd been with Viola. They had checked into a hotel room because Viola had insisted on it. At first, Jalen thought she seemed a little odd, but figured she had an attitude because he had been playing her off. But it was because he had fallen in love with Grant and was willing to give everyone else up.

He'd even had the current new coach of the Detroit Lions pursuing him for a minute. The coach was working for another team at the time and kept trying to get Jalen to go out of town with him, but Grant was all he really cared about. He'd only responded to Viola because she kept blowing his phone up.

Now that he'd played their last rendezvous back in his head, he figured out how Viola had done it. Ordinarily, Viola got off on swallowing his juices, but that day, she'd jumped up and run to the bathroom to spit it out after giving him oral pleasure. She'd made some joke about it being extra salty. She must have spat it into some type of small container.

"PUNK-ASS BITCH!" he shouted, but it still wasn't clear why Viola—or Victor, or whoever the fuck he/she was—would do that to him. Who wanted him out of the way? Jalen was wondering if there was a connection between Victor and Grant. If so, that would have been some dirty shit for Grant to do. To play with his life and his freedom? And for what? Grant had already previously broken it off between them. Even though it had been hard, Jalen had accepted it and moved on.

He wanted answers now, and the only way he was going to be able to get them was from Grant directly. He was sure Viola was nowhere to be found. When Jalen looked at his exoneration papers, they said a government official had produced evidence that cleared him, but there was no name attached. Now Jalen wondered if that government official was Grant Ashford, and if guilt was eating him up for what he'd done. Maybe that was why they'd produced evidence to free him and maybe the check he had from the state for being wrongfully convicted was supposed to be enough to satisfy Jalen. But one hundred dollars a day wasn't going to do it.

He needed answers and he needed to know why a man he'd loved would set him up and send him away. There was a chance Grant didn't have a conscience and Jalen would still be sitting in prison for a crime he hadn't committed. He was allowing his anger to get the best of him, and when he got angry, he got horny and needed attention.

He picked up his phone and texted Taylor first, to see when she would be returning home. She texted she was handling church business and would be home late. He had figured that and made his next call.

"Well, about time you called me back. I want to see you. I wrote you twice a week for three years and I'm the last one to see you as a free man?" the voice on the other end of the phone said.

Jalen knew his friend had a point, but he had come home and was going to try to change his life. One thing he knew for sure was he couldn't change if he continued doing the same things with the same people. He felt he'd owed it to his wife to be real with the marriage, but that had changed after spending half a day with her. She hadn't changed from handling the church business, so he knew wholeheartedly their marriage if they stayed together would be the same.

"It ain't like that, baby. You know I have a few responsibilities elsewhere and I wanted to tend to that, so when I finally got a chance to see you, we wouldn't be interrupted."

It sounded like pure bullshit and it was, but his friend was still loving and hanging on to every word coming out Jalen's mouth. He was just going to act like he was feeding into the game Jalen thought he was running. Besides, he hadn't had anything close to Jalen in his bed since he'd been gone, and that was what he'd really missed. Good sex had its way of working on some folks' souls. Many have sold their souls to the devil for some good pipe. Good sex had Maurice risking his career as a police officer by consorting with a criminal, and he'd even kept money on Jalen's books while he was gone.

"So, since you put it like that, when can we be alone?" Maurice whined.

"I'm free, baby, and surprisingly, my Range Rover is still here. I was hoping Taylor hadn't sold it and she hadn't. I haven't started it since I've been home, but I'm sure my snow-white beauty will fire right up," Jalen replied, laughing.

"If not, you know I can come get you, flashing lights and all. Only this time, you won't be going to that kind of jail. You'll be a prisoner of love," Maurice joked.

"That shit ain't funny, baby, and no, you can't come to my house unless you have a search warrant. But I would suggest you keep that in your possession, so when I get there you can strip search me," Jalen said, having fun with him back.

"Now you're talking my kind of language. My dick is getting hard just thinking about you, baby. Hurry up and get that truck started so we can fire up some other engines. If you're hungry, I'll make something before you get here."

Jalen remembered he'd totally forgotten about the sandwich he'd made. Maurice wanted to cook for him but he really wanted some of Chef Q's famous ribs over at Sterling's BBQ and now that he thought about it, Taylor, his own wife hadn't even offered to cook shit before she'd left; she'd just gotten fucked and gone back to handling the church's business. Every time church business came across his mind, he found himself getting angrier at the fact he'd come home to the same old shit.

He'd just had a notion: He wouldn't need her once the check cleared for his settlement. It was enough money for him to start over and do whatever he wanted to do with his life. If that decision would make anyone happy, he knew for sure her jackleg preacher daddy would be the one.

"Yeah, Moe baby, that sounds good; cook whatever you'd like. Did you do that other favor I asked of you?"

"What was that, baby?"

"I asked you to order a female police uniform. I want to raise that skirt up and break the law."

"You know I did. I even had the shirt custom made."

"All right, give me a minute and I should be on my way."

"Sounds good, and trust me, I'm sure you'll enjoy your late-night dinner. I want you to be looking forward to dessert."

The call ended and Jalen thought, *'Maurice is still the same Maurice.'* The promotion to sergeant in the Detroit Police Department hadn't changed anything about him. He was still over the top, just like he was on the day they had met.

The keys to his truck were on the wall rack which were wooden letters spelling out the word "keys". It was the only thing in the same place in the Ross household. Jalen grabbed his keys and went out the side door to the attached garage.

His truck was still there and in one piece. It didn't appear to have been driven since he had been gone, but he knew someone had to have driven it from the city tow lot back to their house. The day he was arrested, it had been towed for evidence. His wife also must have actually honored his request when he'd first gone to prison and started his truck at least once a month to keep the battery from dying, he thought when the Range fired right up, and filled the gas tank as necessary.

He chuckled as he entered the vehicle when he noticed his favorite leather jacket and Michigan State University hat still laying on the front seat. He picked the jacket up and put it on. It had been oversized when he left, but now it was a perfect fit. He touched the hat and smiled because Viola was a University of Michigan fan and they'd had long debates about the football games. Those were the good ol' days, he thought as he pulled the cap down snugly on his head.

He still couldn't believe he had put together how Viola had set him up by keeping a specimen of his semen, but it was still tricky and amazing to him how a fourteen-year-old girl had gotten on the stand and pointed him out to the jury, saying those awful things about him like he was a pedophile—all the way down to describing his penis and the interior of his truck. Jalen was a lot of things—a cheat, a liar, and even a hustler—but what he *wasn't* was a man who would mess with someone's child.

He figured he could talk to Maurice and run his theory by him. He also wanted to see if there was anything in the original police report that hadn't been mentioned in court. He knew he was going to have to lay the shit on extra thick to get any information out of him though. That light-skinned, pretty-boy, Chris Brown-look behind the badge may have fooled a lot of people, but Jalen could easily tell Maurice Bridges was not a spring chicken. He was very knowledgeable, in addition to being very street savvy. He possessed a lot of game, and on top of that, he knew the power of the badge had most likely gotten him plenty of conquests with whatever his flavor happened to be that day.

Subsequently, Jalen didn't give two fucks about his past life, or his right-now sex life. They were going to eat, fuck and suck each other, and Jalen was going to try to use his manhood to coerce Maurice into giving him the information he needed. He checked his glove box and was surprised Taylor hadn't searched his truck. The box of rubbers he'd left were right there—or, maybe she had and just hadn't cared. He checked the expiration date, and ironically, they expired today.

"LOOK AT THAT! TALK ABOUT FAVOR!" he yelled, mimicking his wife.

"Time to make it do what it do, baby," he said as he hit the Lodge freeway.

All he could think about was getting revenge on Grant Ashford for setting him up. It wasn't called for, and it was a damn shame for someone a person cared about to treat them like that.

"He must have been afraid I was going to out him. That's the only thing that makes sense, but that's okay. Karma is a bitch, and in this case, a down-low bitch!"

Chapter 11

The all-black 944 Porsche with the Targa top pulled up to the front of Vanessa's building. Zach looked up at the high-rise, then back at the address to make sure he was at the right place. He hadn't been home in a few years, but still he knew the area where she stayed wasn't cheap and he wondered when the city had started giving secretaries that kind of money.

Zach drove to the next block and dialed her number. She picked up right away, knowing the unknown caller was him.

"Where are you, baby? My time is limited," Vanessa said.

Zach thought, *'It's Sunday night; where is there to go?'*

"Chill, baby; I'm outside. I just wanted to make sure I was at the right building, If I remember correctly, some of the Detroit Pistons have condos in this same building," he replied to her rushing him.

He really wanted to say, "Chill, bitch. There ain't no need to rush this one-eighty-seven that's about to go down."

"Yeah, baby, that's my building. Come on in and come up to the twenty-first floor."

"That's cool. Ain't no doorman, is it? You know we've both got to keep this shit on the down low," he said, wanting to make sure no one would be able to identify him.

"Actually, Jack, the doorman, doesn't come in until midnight. You'll be satisfied and long gone before he gets here," she replied and smiled, loving her plan.

"Sounds like you're confident, baby, like you've got some mad skills. Just don't let that plump ass sign a check it really can't cash. I think you might be allowing the couple years between us fool you."

"Well, don't talk about it, be about it. You've got the apartment number; ain't nothing between us but air, opportunity and a private elevator that I've already unlocked for you," she stated, slipping on her red outfit—a red nightie, red heels, and red lipstick to match her toenails, which were already painted red.

"I really like you, baby, and I love a shit-talker. I'll see you in a few."

He really did like the way Vanessa talked. She was a bad bitch too, and her imitation-90210 ass had the look of a distinguished attorney, but the language of a hoodrat. She was the worst kind of snake: one who could crawl on her belly in the ghetto jungle when she wanted to, and one who could slither into the elite lives of people like the Ashfords. Those types would sell their souls for a profit, especially a high-end profit.

Zach parked his car a block up, went in the trunk, and retrieved a brown leather bomber jacket and a green Michigan State baseball hat. It wasn't his college, so he didn't care if it was murder apparel. Zach was right at the door when she opened it up after he'd stepped off the elevator. Vanessa couldn't believe he was standing there, looking like his father in the flesh.

'Damn, if Grant wasn't such a fairy, I could've fucked the whole family,' she thought.

"I see you ain't scared," Vanessa said, looking Zach in the face, admiring his soft look that was easy on the eyes.

"Scared? You're serious, aren't you? Only thing I'm scared of, baby girl, is a ghost, and the only reason he can scare me is because I can't see him. See, that gives him an unfair advantage. But anything I can see, I can conquer, or find a way to handle it," he replied, smiling and thinking about the way she looked in her booty-call gear.

He knew she thought she was fly in her little outfit, but little did she know, his boyfriends back at school wore top-of-the-line lingerie like Agent Provocateur, while she was strutting around in Victoria's Secret. He made sure his boys had the best and he took care of his people. That was where he and his father were different. He had read enough letters that day to know his father was a runaway when it came to people and feelings. Zach was just the opposite: If he liked his people, they just had to take a number and wait their turn. Zach was a master manipulator, extremely proficient at playing people in different positions and keeping them in rotation. That was his law, and so far, he was upholding it.

Vanessa loved Zach's swag and almost hated that his mother was coming over right after he left. She had a feeling, that when the lights went off, the young man in front of her might be able to handle his business. She eyeballed the lump behind his zipper, but knew she had been fooled by prejudging trouser lumps before. A few seconds would tell. She used her index finger, motioning for him to follow her into her bedroom.

It was a large and sumptuous bedroom, decorated in bold strokes of red like her outfit, accented with deep metallic-gray borders and white crown molding fixtures dipped with specs of silver. Her circular bed was draped in red satin sheets and sat smack dab in the middle of the room atop a short platform.

The setup was nice and it was the only apartment or condo he had ever been in where three of the bedroom walls were huge windows. The design of the building and her place being a corner condo caused the bedroom to be shaped like a triangle, the top being the entry point. She had an enormous arrangement of white lilies and red roses in a tall-mirrored vase on a pedestal centered in the widest window, the middle one behind the bed.

Zach was wondering if he should just toss her out that window. He wasn't sure how he was going to kill her or how soon. He guessed it depended on how good her pussy was. He was going to let her sensual side determine her death rate. The better she was, the quicker she was going to die. If the sex was bad, he would slowly torture her and tell her stories about how bad her pussy was and that was why his cousin Gary hadn't gotten hard when he use to fuck her. That was a story she would have liked to know. It didn't matter what she found out now about anybody, because where she was going, they didn't gossip, so she couldn't tell another soul she was the one who'd been played all along.

Zach continued to survey her room and one thing he liked about Vanessa was her ability to coordinate. He really loved the décor in her bedroom and truly admired the two painted masterpieces by Ing Donaville resting on easels in the two corners. He hated that he had to kill her because he really wanted to discuss her choice of artwork at that moment.

She pulled him to her huge bed, sitting down on the foot of the bed and pulling him between her legs. She took off his leather jacket first, unbuttoned his oxford shirt, and pulled it from inside his pants. That gave her enough room to slide her hand down the front and see what he was working with. Her eyes bucked two sizes when she had to stand up to grasp the base of the tip, and the girth felt like she was holding a fucking soda can.

"Damn, if you seriously know how to use that thing there, a bitch might pack herself in your suitcase when you leave to go back to school," she said, instantly aroused. Her kitty had gotten wet just from touching it. They hadn't even kissed yet, but she was surely ready to feel his full lips and his tongue play with her tongue.

"Then I guess we need to find out if I'm going to need two people to carry my suitcase then," he replied, easing her body back down to the bed.

It wouldn't be Zach's first female kill, and when he was done with her, she would officially become victim number two. Last year, he had murdered a female student who'd begged him to have sex with her; then she recorded it without his knowledge. There had been a rumor around campus about his sexuality and she'd gone out of her way to prove to the student body that Zach Ashford wasn't gay. It had worked and the rumors had stopped. Months later, when Donna Henderson was found dead in a trash compactor, the authorities never looked Zachery Ashford's way.

Vanessa wanted to go the whole nine yards with Zach, but she figured she didn't have that much time. She anticipated filling her throat with his massive ten-inch cock, but if she started, she knew she wouldn't stop, so she backed down from giving him head.

"Come on, baby, get this pussy," she said loudly, as Zach was now completely naked in front of her.

His body was chiseled and the definition of his biceps showed he worked out regularly. His six-pack made him look like a master weight-builder, and when he slid inside her finally, his first few strokes told the story whether he knew what to do or not.

Since Zach wasn't going to leave this one alive to tell anyone, he went to work on her, banging her insides. He was careful to make sure the two rubbers he had slipped on were tight enough, and he made sure he'd put them on before any pre-cum had surfaced from the tip of his dick. Being pre-med had taught him a lot, and taking his extra-credit course in forensic science had been a plus. All serial killers should take forensic classes online to learn how to commit the perfect murder.

'That's a good idea,' he thought, fucking the shit out of Vanessa.

He could teach an online forensics class for maniacs, even do live videos to tutor his crazy students. They didn't have to know who he was behind a mask. All they would want to know was how to commit the perfect murder. One thing about serial killers, they left clues when they were ready, when they wanted a little heat, because it had become boring to them.

"OH, BABY, ARE YOU FUCKING SERIOUS? I'VE NEVER CUM LIKE THIS, BABY! KEEP FUCKING ME!" Vanessa cried out.

She was enjoying Zach and thinking about how was she going to put Ava off tonight, because she was going to be too damn tired for anymore sex. Zach wasn't losing any speed or timing, and it seemed like every time she came on him, he grew another inch. She was loving it, but wished he would ease up some from his stroke and take some of the pressure off her guts he was trying to rearrange. He didn't say anything while he beat her down inside, just kept hitting it harder and harder.

Vanessa was talkative now, but she knew whenever this young man decided to stop the pounding, she was going to be speechless. She wouldn't be able to talk for trying to catch her breath alone. She had screwed some well-endowed men before in her life, but none of them had pipe like Zach. She wondered right after her next nut if his father was like him, or should she say, if Zach had gotten it from his father. If so, it was a shame all that dick was satisfying a man's anatomy instead of pleasing Ava daily. Hell, he could have even cheated if he was strapped like his son, and no bitch in the country would have ratted him out. One thing in the world that was hard to find was good dick, so when bitches found it, they accepted some of the craziest, off-the-wall shit from a man, just to keep that good dick resurfacing in their lives.

Zachery finally stopped thinking about other shit—like, if his car was okay down the street, had his father landed safely in Washington, and how was his new boo, Logan Allen, doing back at school. He was a little upset because he thought Vanessa had said she had that good-good. It wasn't even just okay. She'd definitely put some miles on this highway. Too many women thought their sex was good because men wanted them and kept coming back, when in all actuality, it was just easy to get and that was the real reason they kept coming back. But enough with this raggedy cunt. It was showtime!

Zach started pumping faster, getting deeper inside her. He knew he had to hurry up because there was no way she was going to get him off. She was starting to dry up, and even with the rubbers on, his shit was starting to irritate a little. He acted his part now, screaming how good the pussy was. He kept her mind preoccupied while he ruffled the sheets enough to disturb the manner her bed had been made. After pulling up the red silky sheet, Zach located a seam and began ripping the sheets as he called out her name. He almost called her Logan, but caught himself.

"You going to cum, baby? Make that dick cum for momma, baby. Come on, you can do it!" she cried out.

He'd had enough and flipped her over, putting Vanessa on her knees. The spaghetti straps to her negligée had slid off her shoulders and her Victoria's Secret garment was around her waist. Originally, Zach had planned to strangle her with the torn sheet, but this seemed more appropriate. On his next upward stroke, he pulled her upward from the back by her neck with one hand and slid the lingerie up around her throat with his other hand, all the while maintaining his stride. Now that was multitasking. He twisted and tightened the knot, but was amazed because the crazy broad was enjoying it like it was a part of the routine.

"Bitch, I'm killing you," he said to her as he watched her buck, grind, and thrust her hips backward into his pelvis.

He pulled and tightened it more, cutting off her air supply, but she still didn't get it and kept twerking her hips at full speed, ready to have a full orgasm.

"I'm killing you," Zach said to her again.

"Yes, you're killing this pussy, baby," she managed to say through clenched teeth.

'Oh my God,' he thought, *'this dumb bitch has a master's degree in criminal justice and doesn't know when someone is choking her to death.'*

She was losing color in her face fast; her air had been completely cut off. Zach didn't know what she thought was happening, but she grinded her hips upward until her very last breath. Amazingly, when it was all said and done, he came and they both had a happy ending. He stood, looking down at her lifeless body, ass up and face down into the bed, and just smiled, wishing he could take a picture. This was truly a work of art, he thought as he chuckled to himself. Zach knew he had to straighten her body quickly before rigor mortis set in.

"I ain't a killer, bitch, but don't push me," he rapped out as he put back on his clothes.

He had on thin, flesh-toned surgical gloves that were so thin she hadn't been able tell he was wearing them. It was a new product designed in Europe and they weren't even available to doctors in the states yet, but the colleges had access to all kinds of test materials.

Once he'd dressed, he wiped her body down, sprayed the bed well with Biogen, saturating it, to remove all traces of DNA, and arranged her corpse neatly in her bed, covering her up and making sure her eyes were closed. He walked over to a desk in her living room and moved the mouse. He punched a few keys on her computer keyboard and her monitor blared brightly back to life. He checked her history, examining everything she had been looking at this past week.

After the system reset was complete, he trashed all her private emails and scrambled the disk drives with another passcode his cousin Gary had given him. It was a blocker that would take the Feds an enormous amount of time to break through. Most of the time, they wouldn't even go through with the timely and costly procedure to investigate, unless it involved a high-ranking official or high-profile case. Surely the death of this tramp wouldn't warrant a federal investigation.

Zach made a mental note to have Gary permanently scrub her cellphone call log when something told him to check her desk drawers, but he didn't find anything. Then he remembered the nightstand in her bedroom. The moonlight vibrantly illuminated the room, and Zach opened the nightstand drawer and struck gold. He found just the materials he was looking for. After folding and tucking the papers inside his back pocket, Zach stood there, briefly admiring Vanessa's beauty basking in the moonlight, before finally deciding to leave.

On his way out the door, Zach texted 9-1-1 from her cellphone after resetting it. In order for their plan to work, her body needed to be found and quickly. He looked around the apartment one more time as he was exiting, stopped, and turned on her radio. Gerald Levert was playing, and all he heard as he walked toward the door was, *"I ain't much on Casanova / Me and Romeo ain't never been friends..."*

He zipped up the bomber jacket and put the Michigan State cap back on just before exiting Vanessa's apartment.

Chapter 12

Walter's private Boeing was in the air now and there was no one on the plane but him, Grant, and the pilot. The two of them sat in the back at a round table, talking and discussing the election. Walter Burke was an average-built man with a full salt-and-pepper beard and a thin mustache that wouldn't grow to connect to his beard. A lot of people said he looked like he could be Lionel Richie's father. Grant could see the resemblance, and sometimes, he would tease him about it to piss him off.

One thing about Walter that was different from most politicians was he knew exactly how to get what he wanted, and Grant had learned that very quickly. It was Walter's letter of recommendation that had gotten Grant's son accepted without hassle into med school, and that had puzzled Grant because Zach Ashford hadn't applied at Walter's alma mater. Somehow, Walter knew people everywhere in the world. He was more like a celebrity than the governor of a state whose economy was failing tremendously.

"Grant, it seems like you don't trust me anymore," Walter said as he continued fortifying himself for the long night ahead by filling his stomach with crab legs.

"What makes you say a crazy thing like that?" Grant replied, raising an eyebrow with sure concern.

When a man like Walter Burke made accusatory comments, one had to be careful of how he or she responded, because they usually came with more than just a beginning and simple ending.

"I mean, if I tell you a duck can pull a truck, don't ask questions. Just hook the duck up to do its job," he said with a diplomatic laugh.

"I get that, but I still don't know why you referenced trust issues. What makes you think I don't trust you, Walter? I mean, I'm here above the clouds with you alone. I walked away from practicing law and I'm damn-near letting you control my career, and I'm sure this isn't the first time you've done this to someone, Walter. So, I must trust you, just like the others did."

"Not the first time? What is that supposed to mean, do tell?" Walter asked, wanting to know exactly what Grant meant or knew.

Walter was one of the brightest stars in the sky when it came to book smarts. When it came to people though, there was no school that could teach the skills he possessed. Walter was so sharp, he could talk a mother into paying for her own breast milk.

"I mean, I know how this lifestyle goes—I've fractured a heart or two before in my day—but when I said not the first time, I meant the first time you've saved a wretch like me," Grant responded, trying to clean up his previous statement.

"You're no wretch, Grant, no, not at all. You're smart, Grant, a smart, beautiful man, but you don't see half the picture because you can't see what the artist is thinking beforehand." Walter smiled as he said it. "I'm doing my best to give you my hand on this journey, Grant. I hope you aren't doing your best to bite it."

Walter continued shoving another piece of meat he had just cracked from another crab leg into his mouth. He made sure the sigh he'd just done was loud enough to be audible so Grant would know it needed a response.

To Grant, it was similar to his life from day one when he'd figured out who he was sexually. Every delicate situation he seemed to get wrapped up in was because he'd lost control of his feelings. He'd learned at an early age not to react to emotions. Allowing your emotions to control your behavior could cause you to respond irrationally. This was one of the main reasons he'd walked away from so many relationships. But he knew Walter Burke well, and Walter was totally up to something. He wondered if he'd found out about him forging his name on the exoneration papers. He'd planned to tell him, but now Grant wanted to wait to see if he knew.

Grant replied to Walter good-naturedly. "I would never bite the hand that feeds me and allows me to feed my family, but I feel like I'm being poked with a double-edged sword here. Like, let's just be frank with each other. We've been everything else, except candid and straightforward."

"Okay, Grant, your wish is my command," Walter said, pushing his plate out in front of him.

He briefly remembered he would have to dispose of the dirty dishes since he'd purposely given his flight staff the night off. He wanted it to be an up-close-and-personal flight with Grant and him, one-on-one.

"Some things are overdue in this world by a millennium or two, and the only way to control the world and get what you want is by controlling the government. You see Detroit is ours and we can do whatever we want with the city. If we want to give a key to the city to a perfect stranger, no one will question us. You know why that is, Grant? Because we make the rules in Detroit.

Now, imagine that type of power in every city in every branch of politics. Can you imagine what the world would be like?"

"You're still talking in riddles. This-millennium-or-two babble, can you be precise?"

"Yes, I can, but Grant, I know it's hard for anyone to understand a demand from a career choice they didn't want to identify with in the first place. I was in the same boat many years ago. Me getting involved in politics took me away from my friends and my family, inconveniently and unpredictably. But I stuck it out. Not out of love for the job at first, but because I could see the bigger picture that was coming down the line. So, I didn't feel persuaded to change because of the inconvenience. Are you starting to get what I'm saying yet, Grant?"

"This sounds like a power trip, Walter, one that could be very dangerous. Are you trying to create a national political network?" Grant replied, thinking he was starting to understand what the governor was trying to convey.

Walter laughed at Grant's naïve mindset. "Exactly! Listen, my dear love bug, every one of us—and when I say every one of us, Grant, I mean men like me and you, powerful decision-making men with the drive and hunger for the pure animal instinct inside us to come out—we have powerful men on the down low working for the government in all different levels. United, we will be able to run the nation, and hopefully, the world."

"So, you're thinking about controlling everything, from the way you're talking. From the smallest assignment straight to the oval office?" Grant asked.

His relationship with Walter Burke was supposed to be a simple relationship for the two of them. In the beginning, Walter had wanted some company and Grant had given him that. In return, Walter had promised Grant he would make him forget all his troubles, which at the time sounded like the best plan Grant had heard in a long time. Now, he was somewhat confused and not sure if his friend and playmate was thinking with a full deck. Because if Walter was saying what Grant thought he was saying, there was no way it could be done.

"Grant, I see the look on your face, and I say, Oh ye of little faith. You think putting the next president in a seat is hard to do? Think again. Every president has been strategically manifested to take the seat. Forget the voting system for a second, only think electoral votes, and think if we start small and work our way up, by the time you run for president in the next four years, we will surely win."

Grant threw his hands up and told Walter he felt like mayor was as far as he wanted to go, but he was sure Walter had more up his sleeve. Grant knew it wasn't going to be easy to get out of a plan Walter thought was foolproof.

"Oh no, Grant, there's no backing out of this one, baby! You're going to put us on the map with this win."

"Wait, Walter; you can't make me run for president in four years. What if I don't want to run? What if I die between now and the next four years?"

"Simple, if you die, which is the only way you won't be running, then we spend the next eight years grooming Zach," Walter said, causing Grant to spit out the water he was sipping on.

"ZACH WHO?! MY SON? ZACHERY ASHFORD? That is the most ludicrous idea I have ever heard." Grant laughed out loud. "Zach has his heart set on medicine, not politics," he added.

"That might be true. Anyone can set their heart somewhere when they aren't aware that a better possibility is out there for them. Now, you tell me Dr. Zachery Ashford wouldn't want to be president of the United States. I'll wait for your reply."

"I don't think politics is his thing," Grant lied with a false innocence. He didn't think Zach had an interest in political per se, but he knew Zach wanted to be influential.

"Well, when you call it politics, it really isn't anyone's thing, but when you call it power, it can become everyone's thing and quickly," Walter said, standing so he could clear the dishes.

The plane was about to land at a private airstrip and Walter felt his cell vibrate, which startled him because he hadn't realized he hadn't turned it off. He retrieved it from his pants pocket and stared with a vulture-like gaze at the number coming across his screen when he recognized it was his brother calling. They both had had similar missions in life, but somewhere along the line, his brother had gotten a calling from God and decided becoming a pastor instead of a politician would better suit him. Walter had argued for three years before giving up on trying to change his brother's mind.

It wasn't until about five years ago, when his niece claimed she was going to marry her boyfriend, Jalen Ross, that Walter's brother had decided he needed to serve a different God, even if it was just temporary. There was no way Walter or his brother wanted Taylor to marry a man who, in their minds, wasn't worthy of cleaning the family toilets.

He decided he wasn't finished with Grant and taking a call could interrupt the vibe between them he'd just strategically set up. Walter knew Grant's head was spinning and he was wondering what Walter was going to say next, but Walter decided to make him wait until they checked in the hotel and had a little fun. Walter looked at his watch and knew Zach should be home, sleeping in his bed by now. He knew he could count on him to do what had to be done.

Sometimes Walter felt like Zach was more his own son and more reliable than his father. He enjoyed getting away and visiting him at college every other month. Zach was one of a kind, and he made sure when Walter showed up that the right party was happening. Walter truly loved satisfying his carnal and libidinous appetite by feeding upon the selection of eager, fervid and sometimes virgin young men Zach bestowed upon him.

They checked into a Marriot hotel, using the app to bypass the front desk and to unlock their doors. The two utilized a fictitious corporate account with rooms booked under assumed names. They always booked two rooms in case any paparazzi got pictures, and it was just safer not to arouse any speculation from cheesy tabloids. Enough scandal was going on in today's news, and neither Walter nor Grant needed to be a part of any of it. They went to their adjoining rooms, and Walter looked at Grant as they held their cellphones to the doors, using the digital keys to enter their rooms.

"Let me freshen up. I'll call you over shortly," Walter said.

Grant just nodded and entered his room. He sat his overnight bag down before plopping down in the soft chair that decorated the room. *'Walter is obviously crazy,'* he thought. There was no way in four more years that Grant was going to enter the presidential race. No way! And nothing Walter said or did was going to change his mind.

In fact, he was thinking about retiring from politics, taking a year off work and fishing the Great Lakes, finding himself and finding out what he had been born to be. He'd tried football and he'd been good at it, but there had been too many complications. Plus, now, he was too old. He'd tried his hand at law and had been good at that as well, until Walter had convinced him to try politics. But he felt this game had triple the trials that playing football or being a lawyer had plagued his life with. Sometimes, he felt like he was in a no-win situation.

"Why?" he asked himself as he buried his head in the palm of his hands, slumping over. "What did I do to deserve this shit?"

Chapter 13

Jalen parked his truck outside his friend's home. Maurice was all right, but Jalen knew his heart wasn't in their relationship. He was fun in bed, but besides that, the two of them had nothing in common. He remembered Maurice kept a spare key for him to use under the welcome mat, and he bent down to pick it up from where it lay. He thought people only did that on TV and in the movies, but to each their own. He just wanted to eat, have some fun, and get back home. It had been late when he'd left and Taylor still hadn't made it back to their home.

"Church business, my ass," he said under his breath as he walked in.

Maurice was in the kitchen, standing listlessly next to the trash can as he disposed of the skins from some potatoes.

"Damn, look at you! You must've been working out the whole time you were there," he said, staring at Jalen.

"Yeah, I was doing a little something; had to keep my mind off being confined to a small-ass room with a funky-ass cellmate I couldn't stand," Jalen replied, thinking quickly for a second about his ex-roommate who was more than likely right about his wife.

She'd probably had her a Jody in the background all the time. The church's business probably consisted of her and Deacon Jody doing more than worshiping together. That was fine with Jalen now that he was home and had money coming in a day or so. He planned to trade in his Range Rover, buy a new car, get his own place, and fix it up very nice.

Maurice was struggling to finish cooking as he couldn't keep his eyes off Jalen's new muscular body.

"So, are you just going to stand there looking like you've seen a ghost, or are you going to come show a brother some love? You got that promotion and now you're acting brand new, huh?" Jalen said playfully.

"Shit, big boy, I was just sizing you up. They say, when one muscle grows, all of them start to grow," Maurice replied, smiling and stepping to Jalen.

They embraced each other and shared a long, deep, and passionate kiss. Maurice had really missed Jalen and wanted to show him with a brief moment of passion.

"Whatever you're cooking sure smells good," Jalen said, releasing Maurice.

"I'm sure the aroma of any home-cooking would beat them damn hook-ups they make in the joint," Maurice replied. "But, if you'd like to know, it's grilled lamb chops, with sautéed asparagus, garlic mashed potatoes, homemade rolls, and caramel apple cheesecake for dessert," he said, grabbing an oven mitt to remove the final touch of dinner from the oven.

"Instead of a cop, baby, you should have been a chef."

"I still can be, but cooking is second nature. It doesn't bring the adventure like police work. I couldn't stand the heat all day and do it for a living. Besides, you don't know how excited I get when I'm chasing a suspect and he's wearing tight jeans. I anticipate frisking him; then it makes me think about you."

"Yeah, yeah, tell me anything, Maurice. Now that sounds like some good-ass game you're running this time," Jalen said as he looked around. "I like what you did in the living and dining rooms. Maybe you can decorate my new place."

"I'd love too, but wait... You're moving?" Maurice replied in a flirty tone.

"Yes, I am. It's time for me to live my life. I really like the floors."

"Oh, the hardwood floors—yeah, I got a really good deal, and besides, the guy who installed them was pleasant on the eyes."

"You know something? You're just a horny little bitch, ain't you?"

"Let's taste this food; then I will show you better than I can tell you," Maurice said, fixing them both a plate.

Jalen removed his brown leather bomber jacket and sat his green Michigan State hat on the counter. He grabbed a Corona beer out the fridge and sat at the table. One of the things he liked about Maurice was he showed a lot of hospitality. He would always stick a napkin in Jalen's shirt before he ate. Nothing had changed. He did it again, planting a soft peck on Jalen's lips.

"I'm happy to know some good things don't change," Jalen said, slapping Maurice on his ass. "Hey, it seems like you've tightened up some too back there!"

"Well, I had to go through six weeks of retraining, and it was awful, baby. I was sore every night and no one here to help me work off the pain."

"There your ass goes, running game again. I'm sure you pulled out that little black book and saw a few names you'd given a break to specifically for the purpose of one favor deserves another favor."

"Look at you. You think you know me, don't you? I tell you it was tempting, but every suspect I surveyed couldn't measure up to you. I hope you don't make me out to be a liar."

"There you go, trying to inflate a brother's ego," Jalen replied, taking down half his beer with one chug.

They began eating dinner and Maurice noticed Jalen had gotten quiet on him. He looked up to see he was lost in his own reverie, a bittersweet one by the look on his face.

"What's wrong, boo? Have you ever gone to a friend's house to eat and the food just ain't no good?" Maurice rapped.

"I mean the macaroni's soggy, the peas are mush, and the chicken tastes like wood," Jalen rapped back, and they laughed. *Rapper's Delight* was one of their favorite songs.

"But for real, you don't like the food?"

"The food is delicious. It's just there have been some things bothering me all day and I can't shake them from my head. You ever have something, I mean some shit, in your head, that you know happened, but you have no real proof?"

"You know my occupation, so of course I can attest to having been there on several occasions. What is it? What's got you so fricking mind-boggled?"

"My case for one."

"Why are you worried about that now? You're free! You were exonerated and you're getting paid. Seems like you got another chance, Hurricane. You remember that movie with Denzel Washington? Not many people get a second chance, Jalen."

"Thanks for the encouraging words, Dr. Phil, but I'm serious about this. I'm free, but how? Think about it. Why now? Why right before Grant Ashford announces he is running for mayor?"

"You still on that whole Grant Ashford thing? I thought I was enough to make you forget about him," Maurice replied, a little sad Grant's name had surfaced.

"I'm not interested in Grant's other life anymore; that's something I let go of a long time ago," he lied. "I just think I've figured it out. I think I know how my DNA got inside that child."

"What are you talking about? You sound crazy as hell. We both know how your DNA got inside her. I think you need to understand that we all have certain fetishes we can't control Jalen. You were creeping around with the girl's foster father and you got curious; just let that shit go. She was probably fast as hell, and I assumed you didn't know she was only fourteen years old. Shoot, my great grandmother got married at fourteen," Maurice said, getting irritated that Jalen was the only one who didn't realize he was guilty. DNA hadn't been wrong since it had been introduced into the court system, so why did Jalen think anyone would believe him when his DNA said he'd had sex with that girl.

Jalen was pissed. He slammed his fist on the table and stood up. "WHAT THE FUCK?! ARE YOU SERIOUS RIGHT NOW?! YOU *REALLY* THINK I HAD SEX WITH HIS DAUGHTER? I TOLD YOU I'VE NEVER MET HER AND MY FIRST TIME SEEING HER WAS IN COURT!" Jalen yelled, his nose turning red and water pooling in the corners of eyes.

"Damn, I'm sorry, baby. Calm down, and yes, I really did think that. How do you explain your DNA being inside her?"

Jalen started pacing the room. He really wanted to punch Maurice in his face right now, but he didn't deserve that. He had been nothing but good to him. Jalen stopped pacing, got his thoughts together, and replied, "Someone set me up, Maurice. Victor saved my semen from his mouth and inserted it inside that girl, but he couldn't have done it alone. He had no reason to send me to jail. It had to be Grant. Who else would benefit from me going away?"

"Wow! Okay, Jalen, that sounds a bit farfetched, but I believe you. Do you really think he would have inserted your semen, then have his daughter lie? That is very invasive and not to mention disgusting. From your penis to his mouth to whatever he put it in, then in her vagina? And what if she'd gotten pregnant? What kind of father would do that?"

They looked at each other thinking, when Maurice had an epiphany. "THE LAB!" he yelled.

"What about the lab?" Jalen asked, but just as the words left his mouth, he instantly caught on.

Maurice was so excited, like he'd just solved a case. "That's it, baby! Your DNA was never in her. Having his daughter lie is one thing, but I just can't see a father inserting your semen. I bet he just gave it to the diagnostics laboratory."

"Damn, that's probably it. Can you find out the name of the lab? I need to go there and ask some questions."

"Baby, you can't just waltz in there and start asking questions," Maurice responded as he walked over to his laptop and powered it on. Just as the screen came to life, he said, "But wait, you didn't use protection? We always use protection. You fucked a whore raw?"

Jalen sighed. One, because the whole situation was becoming mentally exhausting, and two, because he wasn't in the mood for Maurice to be getting in his feelings about him having sex with another man.

"Oral, Maurice, and we don't use protection when you give me head. The last time Victor and I hooked up, he ran to the bathroom to spit it out; he said it was too salty."

"Well, it is," Maurice joked, but Jalen gave him an irritated look because he failed to find the humor in his response at the moment.

Maurice felt the tension and began to peck away at his keyboard. After a few seconds, he said, "I hate that I can't think of the name. We've used the same lab for years. They submit a bid for a five- or ten-year contract. Okay, here it is. This is who we use. Oh my goodness, baby! I think you were set up!" He pointed to the name of the DNA lab on the screen.

"BURK LABORATORIES? YOU'VE GOT TO BE KIDDING ME!" Jalen yelled.

"See, baby, even though I hate to say it, it wasn't Grant after all."

"I know my father-in-law hates me, but damn, he's a pastor!"

"Sometimes, those are the worst ones..."

"Damn, but Pastor Burk? Do you think my wife was in on this too?"

"I don't know, baby, but I'm wondering how Victor and Pastor Burk know each other?"

"Yeah, I didn't even think about that. Okay, I know who set me up now, but what I don't know is how Victor got his daughter to go along with it. How can you talk a kid into getting on the witness stand and telling a damn lie? That is what's got me puzzled. And why would Victor do this to me?"

"That sounds possible, Jalen, but why? Why would Victor do this to you? What would he have to gain?"

"That is something I just can't figure out. The pastor must have paid him a lot of money to coerce him into doing something as low down as this. I wonder if there was something in the police report that was missed. This damn city is full of crooked-ass people, and somehow, they seem to always get voted in by the people."

Maurice knew Jalen would have to go soon and he hadn't slaved in the kitchen to discuss this case all night, so he decided to change the mood. "Well, this calls for a celebration. I will clean the kitchen later. Baby, you seem like you need a release. Give me a second. Grab yourself another beer and relax; take a load off your feet and some of them clothes off your body. We can at least fix one of your problems," Maurice stated, getting up and walking to his bedroom.

Jalen took him up on the beer offer and removed his shirt before heading back into the living room and sitting on the couch. A few moments later, Maurice re-appeared wearing the police skirt and the custom shirt he'd had made especially for Jalen—well, it was supposed to have been for Jalen. But the last day the floor installer had worked, he'd gotten a chance to see it on Maurice first, and with no regrets from Maurice. He just hated the floorman had moved his business to Atlanta. They could have had a lot of fun together.

"Now, isn't this better?" Maurice asked as he straddled Jalen.

He picked up the remote and turned on some music to change the mood in the room. Jalen put aside his case for a moment and got involved with the task at hand. Maurice slid down between his legs, undoing his zipper and releasing Jalen's penis from captivity.

"Now, let me see if I can make you think about rainbows and butterflies," he said, inserting Jalen's large, swollen rod deep down his throat.

His warm mouth made Jalen finally close his eyes and let it go for a moment. Jalen ran his fingers through Maurice's naturally-curly hair as he directed his head in an up-and-down motion.

"Don't cum in my mouth; I want it all inside me," Maurice exclaimed, stopping for a second to speak his piece.

Jalen heard him, but he quickly pushed Maurice's head back down to complete what he had started.

Jalen didn't ordinarily participate in unprotected anal sex, but he knew he'd better oblige Maurice's request, because that was the only way he was going to talk him into taking care of his needs. He needed to see an official copy of the police report. He had heard rumors while being locked up that the Detroit police sometimes made two reports: the one that was pre-court and the one that went in the file after they got their conviction.

'Could a pastor be this damn devious?' he thought.

His anger was building as his dick was stiffening. He stood Maurice up, turned him around lifting the skirt up, and bent him over the arm of the couch. Maurice had him so wet they didn't even need any lubricant. Jalen instinctively grabbed the condoms from his jacket pocket, but Maurice stopped him.

"You've been gone so long. I want you to cum inside me," Maurice purred.

Jalen obliged and slid into Maurice's anal canal. The pain throbbed with each beat of Maurice's heart as Jalen went to work behind him. He clenched the pillows on the couch and begged for more. Jalen was pumping inside him so hard that his thighs were making red marks on Maurice's ass cheeks and the clapping noise sounded like thunder. Suddenly, he was ready to pop, and he started shaking, still full of juices from his vacation.

"Uggghhhhh," Jalen moaned as if he were in pain.

"I feel it, baby. It's warm... Oh, it's so warm!" Maurice cried out as Jalen collapsed on his back, making him fall face forward into the couch. They were both panting and trying to catch their breath before they spoke.

"Damn, baby, that was amazing. It was everything I hoped and dreamed it would be," Maurice said.

"I have to admit it, you've still got that good stuff."

"So, is that a proposition for round two?" Maurice smiled.

"Maybe, maybe not."

"No fair, Jalen. Don't play with me," he said, using one of the soft pillows to pop Jalen upside his head. "Why maybe not? You name it, whatever you want, baby. If you fuck me again like that, I will be your personal servant."

"Oh, you think you can handle my wishes, huh? Well, you want round two, and I want to see the official police report from my file."

"That's it? That's all you want for some more of that good dick? Give me a second," Maurice said, jumping up and running to get his laptop on his tiptoes, his police skirt still hiked up around his waist.

"Shit, I can take care of that right now," he said as he plopped back on the couch and logged in. "Thank goodness for technology."

Maurice quickly logged on, and now with his promotion, he had unlimited access to data that regular beat cops and petty detectives had to obtain permission to see.

"Ahh, here we go—Jalen Ross."

Jalen leaned to look at the screen and saw his name with big, bold black letters that said "Convicted". Maurice opened the file and began looking at it as Jalen peered over his shoulder.

"Something looks weird here, and here is something else I don't remember hearing at your trial," Maurice said, sounding excited.

"First of all, it says here the girl suffered from severe ADHD and was heavily medicated every time she was interviewed by the arresting officer," he said, scrolling back up, looking at the arresting officer's names again. "John Poe was the arresting officer and the one who filed the first report, but what I find strange here is that Olivia Canton—which was her maiden name, now Olivia Poe—did the official second report. You know, that report your friends talked about in the joint?"

"You mean the after-conviction one that goes in the file?"

"You've got it, but what is really ironic is, shortly after your case, John Poe was transferred to the detail for Governor Burke, who is the brother of your father-in-law, who is the pastor who married John and Olivia. They divorced a few months after you were sentenced. I mean it could all be a coincidence; we both know people fall in and out of love daily."

"What exactly is that supposed to mean, people fall in and out of love daily?"

"Well, after John took the assignment, his marriage to Olivia didn't last long. She divorced him, took back her maiden name of Canton, and told everyone in the district she'd divorced because he was a cheater. You were in jail longer than they were married. That girl is surely a good catch for the right man. I can't believe he divorced her."

Jalen was processing Maurice's statement, when it hit him.

"Wait a minute! Did you just say Pastor Burk and Governor Burke *are brothers*?"

"Yeah, you didn't know that? Rumor is, something happened when they were younger and the pastor wanted to disassociate himself from his brother, so he changed the spelling of his last name by dropping the 'e'."

"Get the fuck out of here! I've been married to Taylor for five years and she's never mentioned that. The governor is her fucking uncle?! Unbelievable."

"She probably didn't mention it because she didn't want you to slip up and mention it. I heard years ago that he fired his entire staff because one employee asked him about it."

"Brothers? They look like night and day."

"They have different fathers. The governor is the oldest, and when their mom remarried, the pastor's dad adopted Walter and changed his name."

"Wow! Thank you, Maurice. I really appreciate your help with all of this."

"Well, baby, now you know everything. I kept my word, so it's time for you to keep yours," Maurice said, fawning over the new look Jalen's body had taken on and the way he worked it.

Jalen snapped out of his thoughts, and although having sex was the last thing on his mind, he knew he might need Maurice again.

"Good job, bitch. Now come here and let daddy make good on his promise."

Chapter 14

Ava pulled up to Vanessa's apartment building. She was livid that she wasn't answering her calls or responding to her text messages. She was ready to give her a piece of her mind when she noticed the array of police vehicles and news reporters who were outside the building as well. She parked her Infiniti truck where she could and got out to go see what all the commotion was about. There was also a group of spectators behind the yellow tape, waiting to see what had transpired. It was a really nice neighborhood and not much crime went on around there, surely, nothing major.

"What's going on?" she asked an elderly woman who was watching the action.

The woman looked at Ava as she rubbed her poodle that was trying to keep warm. "They aren't saying anything yet, but it doesn't look like a housewarming party, that's for sure."

"You're right about that," Ava replied, trying Vanessa's phone again and still getting her voicemail.

A young detective was walking around with a flashlight like he was looking for something outside. Ava thought maybe it was a break in and they were looking for footprints. She remembered Vanessa telling her that, on Sundays, the night doorman came in late. So, maybe someone knew the building's routine and had taken advantage of it.

"EXCUSE ME!" Ava called out, waving to the detective.

He looked up and was going to ignore the nosy person, but they didn't have any leads as far as he knew and just maybe the nosy person had some pertinent information that could be used. He would love to be the first one with a clue. While his boys were inside scanning video footage, he figured, if he got the break in the case, he would look over-competent, while his cohorts looked stupid.

"Yes, ma'am, do you have something you want to tell me?" he asked, squinting his eyes at Ava, searching her face for recognition.

"That was what I was going to ask you. My husband's secretary lives in this building. I was driving past on my way home from a bridge game and saw all the emergency vehicles."

"Oh yeah, now I remember where I saw the deceased. She was on television today at the halftime show. You're Ava Ashford, the councilman's wife, right? The T-shirt lady?"

"Yes, that's me. Did you just say *deceased?*'

"That is correct, Mrs. Ashford. The ligature marks around her neck says the cause of death was strangulation. We figure it had to be someone she knew because there were no signs of forced entry or robbery, and all of her valuables were still intact," the young eager detective said, disclosing too much information. "Do you know where your husband is? We are going to need a statement from him."

"No, well, actually yes. He's on a plane, heading to Washington with the governor for a morning meeting."

"Well, I'm sorry for his loss, but I'm sure we will find the perp. No one commits the perfect crime," he said, turning around and walking off.

He turned back around because he was going to say to Ava that he wanted to be sure to receive a T-shirt when they were available. Grant was his favorite politician and he wanted to support his run for mayor, but Ava had disappeared into the night.

Clyde Byrd tried to get Ava's attention as she turned away and hurried down the street. She got into her vehicle, pulled off, then pulled into a deserted parking lot a couple of blocks away. The tears flowed, transforming her perfectly-applied mascara into black streams down her face, making her look like she was on her way to a Halloween party instead of a date with her boo. She knew Grant also would be crushed by this extreme turn of events. She had to call him and give him the bad news, no matter how bad the timing was. It was late and she knew they should have landed by now. Ava dialed her husband's phone number and it went right to voicemail.

"DAMN IT! NO ONE IN THE WORLD IS PICKING UP THEIR DAMN PHONES TONIGHT!" she screamed at her screen.

Ava wanted to be the one to tell Grant, not have him see it on the morning news. She tried one more time and got his voicemail again. She gave up and headed home to take a hot bath and drink a bottle of wine. There was nothing else she could do.

Washington, D.C. ...

Grant stepped into the shower, inching up the temperature. The water felt good on his sore muscles which hadn't been that way before he'd spent the two hours in Walter's suite. He didn't know what had gotten into Walter, but it was like he had fallen into a fountain of youth and had a point to prove. Grant was used to Walter being the gentle type, but for some reason tonight, he was anything but gentle.

What had pissed Grant off was the conversation they'd continued afterward. Grant just wanted to go to sleep so they could return home soon, but Walter was stuck on preparing him for his future, and it still seemed like he had no say in whatever Walter was preparing. He'd kept his unsympathetic attitude toward Grant's position and being played like a puppet was what bothered Grant more than anything. He didn't like being in company that was one-sided; that always made for a terrible friendship.

It was really late and he didn't want to think about it anymore; Grant just wanted to get some rest. He was starting to think the whole political experience was not what he'd expected and not what he really wanted after all. Walter kept telling him to just watch, it was all going to work out. Grant wasn't too sure about those words. They'd never seemed like threats before, but "just watch" seemed like a threat now.

Grant just wanted to get back home and see his family. He climbed in the bed in his suite alone, looking at the clock on the nightstand. Two hours would be all he had before it was time to head back to the airport.

Chapter 15

Monday, October 3rd...

Jalen woke up early as hell. He was still on prison time in his head. He threw his feet over the side of the bed, touching the floor, and looking back over his shoulder at Taylor, who was still asleep. He decided to take a hot shower and re-entered their bedroom just as his wife was turning over, opening her eyes, and squinting because the morning sun was shining brightly through the blinds.

"Good morning. Would you like for your husband to make you breakfast in bed?" Jalen asked, trying to feel Taylor out. He knew what the answer was going to be before he'd asked; he just wanted to be sure.

"No, I'm okay. We have a ten o'clock meeting at the church this morning. My father said I needed to be there because he can't make it," she replied, getting up and stretching.

"Oh, okay, I get it. You've got to handle church business again today."

"Jalen, why do you say it like that? I take enough static about you from my father. He is always saying a man who finds a wife finds a good thing, but that good thing can't be too good if that man hasn't found God."

"And what exactly does the good reverend mean by that? I do believe in God, probably more than most of the members at your church. I just don't go because it isn't all about a fashion show to me—people with their well-to-do egos, thinking they're better than everyone else, looking down on the less-fortunate people they're sitting next to. I remember the last time I went to church with you, the woman sitting next to me questioned me when I was giving my offering. I put ten dollars in the basket and she looked at me like I was taking ten out. Fuck that! Those folks ain't real Christians."

"I'm sorry you feel like that, honey."

"Sorry? *You're sorry?* I've done my best to clean up my act, as far as the streets are concerned. I know that's still somewhat of a big mess and I'm sure you know some Scripture for it, but in the real world, nothing happens overnight. Sometimes, it may even take longer than you think when a person has personal issues going on."

"Like I said, Jalen, I'm sorry you feel like that, but honestly, things haven't been the same for me either. I think it's about time we call a lawyer. I want a divorce."

"So, you're ready to leave, just run out on me like that? You know I figured something like this was coming. Go on, keep being daddy's little girl all your life. That man ain't going to be happy until he handpicks the puppet that's fucking you, if he hasn't already done so in my absence."

"How dare you speak to me like that in my house?"

"Your house? Oh, this is all you, huh?"

"Well, it's the church's money that pays for everything in and around here. You haven't given me a penny for a bill in three years."

"For real? Three years, huh? Did you forget where I was the last three years? Oh, let me remind you: *in prison for something I didn't do!* And what have you been doing while I was gone? Oh, I know; I don't even know why I asked. You've been taking care of church business," he replied, being condescending.

Jalen stood and quickly dressed, throwing back on the clothes he'd had on last night, and walked to a closet, taking his duffle bag with him. He realized his clothes were in boxes, and just a few of his items were hanging up. He assumed Taylor had packed up his things, and him arriving home a day early had prevented her from completing the task of putting his clothing back. At the moment, that was fine with him.

He stuffed his duffle bag as full as he could and picked up one of the boxes, sitting his bag on top. He had an early appointment to meet with his attorney to pick up his check for being wrongfully convicted. His first thought was he should just take the money and move down south with his cousins. That way, he knew he could have a fresh start, but for some reason, he felt that before he did anything, he had to stay around and get to the bottom of what had really happened to him and who was behind it.

"Oh, so you're leaving? Just like that? Fine, but leave your house key on the counter on the way out."

"Shit, you don't have to say it twice, and make sure you call that lawyer you're talking about. I'm out of here," he said, walking out the bedroom, down the flight of stairs through the kitchen to the garage.

He jumped in his truck and peeled out the driveway like he was racing in the Grand Prix after they'd waved the checkered flag. A part of him wanted to cry because he did have love for her, but the part that didn't want to shed tears felt a big relief, like a weight of pretending he was someone he wasn't had been lifted off his shoulders.

Jalen decided to drive to Maurice's house, hoping to catch him before he went to work, and if he wasn't there, he was sure Maurice would be okay with him using the key to let himself in to chill for a moment to gather his thoughts. Plus, he realized, after getting dressed, that he hadn't replaced the key under the doormat last night and it was still in his pants pocket. Jalen turned on to Maurice's street and noticed an unmarked police car in his driveway. Jalen shook his head, assuming Maurice was having a morning rendezvous.

'Damn, I was just there a few hours ago. He couldn't possibly be that horny,' he thought.

After taking a deep sigh and driving around for about fifteen minutes, Jalen decided to drive downtown. He pulled up to the attorney's office, but it was too early to meet, so Jalen had to figure out his next move. He removed his leather coat, threw it in the back of the truck, and turned his baseball cap to the back. He opened the glove compartment and removed a piece of paper with an address Maurice had given him. It was a little early to be showing up at a stranger's house, but they say the early bird catches the worm, so he wanted to see if that saying applied to snakes too.

Fifteen minutes later, Jalen exited the Davison freeway and was only a few blocks from his destination. When he arrived, he sat outside for a few seconds, wondering if it was cool to be doing his own investigation. It was still heavy on his heart when he thought about his conviction being overturned, stating that information from a high-ranking official had been produced to clear him. No matter how crazy it seemed, he was going to go forward with his own investigation.

He exited the truck and walked to the front door to ring the bell. After ringing it and getting no response, Jalen peeked into the closest window near the door and noticed a television on with the movie *Chocolate Kiss* playing in the front room. He remembered the movie because he was watching it when the police had come to his home to arrest him. He knocked on the door again, then looked at the time on his cellphone, thinking maybe it was too early because no one had come to the door. He remembered Maurice said Olivia worked third shift, so it was possible she was asleep. He was about to leave, when he turned around and saw a forty-caliber Glock staring him dead in the face.

"Turn back around and put your hands up!" Olivia was just returning from her morning jog and her adrenaline was on ten.

"Hey, I was just looking for the person who lives here to talk to her," Jalen confessed.

"Why in the fuck were you peeping through my windows? To me, that looks like you were casing my place. Who sent you?"

"No one sent me, Olivia. You don't know me personally, but if you allow me to put my hands down, I can explain. I'm Jalen, Jalen Ross," he said and apologized for being rude by looking through her front window.

As soon as he said his name, she knew exactly who he was. She lowered her gun and took out her front door key.

"Come in," she said, her mood instantly changed.

Jalen followed Olivia into her home. It was nothing fancy, but you could tell it was a woman's place and it had been decorated on a cop's salary. Jalen observed the far wall above the fireplace and saw all the pictures of the dedicated law officials who were a part of her family.

"Wow, is there anyone in your family who isn't a cop?" he asked.

"Very observant, Mr. Ross, but actually, I had a little brother who died in college. He was going to be a federal agent—well, that's what he wanted to be, but he died from a brain aneurism that the doctors found too late."

"I'm sorry to hear that," Jalen said in a sincere tone.

"It's okay; it's been a long time now. So, what do I owe the pleasure of your visit, now that you're a free man?" she asked.

"You did the official report that went in my file after I was sentenced. I know how the system works, where they have been falsifying reports to receive convictions on people without proving true guilt."

"Wait, are you saying I did something wrong, Mr. Ross?"

"No, not at all. I'm just saying that's how the system works, but that's neither here nor there. Your husband—"

"Ex-husband... go on."

"John Poe was the arresting officer, but his report wasn't even in my file. His report contained information that wasn't made available to my attorney. I didn't know anything about this young girl having severe ADHD and being on prescription meds."

"You're right, Jalen, but I don't know what was going on with your case. I will be the first to admit, there are some shady crime-fighting techniques used in this city by law enforcement officers. You do not have the right to remain silent, and you are guilty until proven innocent," she said, crossing her legs.

Jalen's phone started to ring; he looked at the screen and saw it was his wife.

"This is my wife; we had a fight this morning. Can you give me a second to answer this?"

"Of course. Do you need some privacy?"

"Not at all. I'm a guest in your home; this should only take a minute. I'm sure she's just got another demand or two she wants to throw in my face."

"Yes, Taylor, what is it? I'm a little busy," Jalen said, answering the phone.

"You move fast, don't you?"

"You know what? Fuck you! In fact, don't call my phone until the court date," he said, hanging up on her.

Olivia heard the name, and it was right at that moment that she started putting two-and-two together. Jalen's last name was Ross. His wife, or soon to be ex-wife from the sound of what she just heard, her name was Taylor, Taylor Ross. Her name was not in the police report, either one of them, but Olivia knew the name of the woman her husband was cheating with, and it was Taylor.

Jalen, observing Olivia in deep thought, waved his hand in front of her face, bringing her back.

"So, why exactly did you say you were here looking for me again?"

"I just found it weird that John Poe was promoted to the governor's detail right after I was arrested, and during my trial, the arresting officer couldn't be present because he was working on the campaign trail with his new boss. They used a sworn statement from him, which helped convict me."

"This is crazy, Mr. Ross. As I listen to you, the pieces of this are starting to fall into place. Something you think is completely innocuous can be twisted and made to look incriminating!" she exclaimed.

"What does that mean?"

"Come into the kitchen. Would you like a glass of juice? I have something I think you may need to see."

Jalen followed her through the dining room to the kitchen, wondering what it was. He didn't know if finding out the truth was as necessary as it had been ten hours ago.

"Have a seat," she insisted, shuffling through one of the drawers.

A couple of moments later, Olivia produced and handed a picture of two people to Jalen. He knew one very well and one by mishap.

"This is my wife, Taylor, and John Poe, the cop who arrested me," he said, raising his head to look at her.

"Yes, and she's also the woman I caught my husband cheating with a few years ago. So this proves you were set up, but why? Your wife could have simply filed for divorce and Joe could have just left me as well. Why were you the scapegoat? There has to be something deeper here. One thing that gets me though is, how was your DNA inside the little girl? Now I'm assuming Taylor must have given them your semen," Olivia said as she retrieved two drinking glasses from a cabinet, opened the fridge, and poured them each a glass of orange juice, intently listening to Jalen.

"Nope, and I'm not sure I should answer that. No disrespect, but it was your work that played a part in convicting me."

"I assure you that I had no idea. I may have been a pawn, just as you were. I was fired several months ago when I asked John for a divorce after I discovered he was cheating on me. At the time, I had no idea she was your wife," she replied, looking at the picture.

"Damn, somebody in this town is well-connected and I think I know who it is, but to answer your question," he replied, lowering his head, knowing, that if he was going to be truthful, he had to openly admit he'd had a fling with a transsexual.

"I was going through some things in my relationship with my wife, and it had been going on for a while with Taylor. She was always too busy for me, handling church business and neglecting her duties as a wife. So, one day I ventured out. It started with strip clubs and led to me picking up women. I was cruising and saw this tall chick I figured I could get a blow job from, but the chick turned out to be a man. Honestly, I don't know what drove me back to see this person again and again, but I think he was used to collect my semen."

"Interesting, Mr. Ross, and that's crazy that they honestly had your DNA. I know for a fact the district attorney only had testimony from a specialist that the DNA was a match."

"Yeah, I remember her, Doctor Carrie Solomon."

"You mean, Doctor Carrie Solomon-Burk?"

"*Burk? Are you serious?*"

"Yep. She's the pastor's first wife. Rumor is, she had some type of secret about him cheating and part of their divorce agreement was him allowing her to keep his last name. That's probably how she keeps winning the bids with the city for DNA testing. She owns Burk Laboratories and her company tests for various levels of law enforcement across the state.

"Did you know they never entered a rape kit into evidence and your lawyer never asked for the results? I thought that was odd. Everyone just ran with the fact that your DNA was supposedly inside this child. They said your lawyer was looking for a deal before he even thought about filing a motion to suppress the evidence. Seems like you were sold out all across the board."

"At first, I thought it was Grant Ashford, but I can't believe he would go this far to bury me. It looks like it was Pastor Burk, but that doesn't make sense to me, Olivia. I mean he could have gotten rid of me by just paying me to leave his daughter. That would have been the easiest thing to do. From what I've learned and what you've told me, this is all a bit extreme for a man who simply hates his son-in-law. There has to a be another reason the governor would be involved in this too. How is he benefiting from me going to prison?"

"I don't know, but my husband works for the governor now, and I'm willing to bet that promotion and new assignment was in exchange for some type of favor. Did you know Walter is related to your wife's father? Did you know they are brothers? A lot of people don't know that."

"Yeah, I just found out. All these years and I never put two-and-two together. Her father changed the way he spelled Burke; he dropped the 'e' on the end and goes just by Pastor Burk, no 'e'. There is a chance here that Grant Ashford never knew what was going on, but he is boys with the governor and it's rumored Governor Burke is his biggest supporter for his mayoral race."

"I remember John used to talk about, eight-to-ten years from now, things are going to be different, that he was helping to make a change that was going to come soon enough. I still don't know what he meant, but I can guess it has something to do with Mr. Ashford running for mayor. I've always steered clear of politics, but wait a minute... I do recall him talking about a good deed the church had done for the young girl who was supposedly molested by you."

"Oh, and what was that?"

"He was talking one night while he was drunk. They have a secret club he attends, where all the upper-echelon, elite members, top-flight businessmen, politicians, and athletes are a part of this club, and I remember John saying his new church home had donated twenty thousand dollars to help relocate the girl and her father to another city. He didn't say where, but he did say they were no longer in Detroit."

"That was done in case these people ever had a change of heart. Even cowards have a conscience," Jalen said.

He knew he had to get in touch with Grant Ashford somehow, but Grant wouldn't want to speak to him, he thought as he downed the glass of juice.

"Well, Olivia, you have been a big help to me this morning," Jalen said as she escorted him to the front door.

As they were headed to the door, a breaking news story flashed across the television as a reporter excitedly delivered the news.

"The secretary of mayoral-candidate Grant Ashford was found strangled to death in her apartment last night. Police have one potential suspect who is still at large," the reporter stated.

Jalen knew now it was going to be even more difficult to get to Grant Ashford. He remembered the sound of her voice when he use to call the office and she had refused his calls every time. When he saw her on television yesterday, he'd assumed she was the secretary.

'What a shame,' he thought. She was beautiful and her voice matched her face.

Jalen looked at Olivia, mumbled thank you, and walked to his truck to head to his lawyer's office.

Chapter 16

Grant had been back at least thirty minutes. When he made it home to his house, the front yard was crawling with reporters and there was one marked police vehicle there. He didn't know what the hell was going on, but he figured something big must have been brewing for that much traffic to be invading his privacy.

"THERE'S THE COUNCILMAN RIGHT THERE!" one of the reporters screamed out. Every one of them hightailed it in Grant's direction, trying to be the first one to get his statement or a comment on the murder that had taken place.

"COUNCILMAN, HAVE YOU FOUND A REPLACEMENT FOR MS. JONES YET?" one reporter yelled.

"IS THE CITY GOING TO PAY FOR HER BURIAL?" another reporter shouted.

"GRANT, WHERE WERE YOU LAST NIGHT WHEN YOUR SECRETARY WAS STRANGLED TO DEATH?" Clyde Byrd yelled from the crowd of reporters.

That last question made it clear what was going on. Vanessa was dead and apparently she had been murdered, but who in the hell would murder Vanessa? It had to be a mistaken identity, Grant thought.

"Sorry, everyone, I can't comment now. This is the first I've heard of this tragedy. I shall prepare to speak with the press shortly from my office," Grant said as a tear formed in his eye.

It was unbelievable he was just with her hours ago, dropping her off at her apartment and thanking her for all she did to make his life easier. Now she was gone, dead, strangled. It had to be a mistake. A single officer warded off the reporters so Grant could enter his home and check on his family.

"OKAY, PEOPLE, BACK UP! LET THE COUNCILMAN THROUGH. YOU SEE HE IS JUST AS SHOCKED AS EVERYONE ELSE HERE," the cop said.

Grant thanked him and rushed inside. He knew Ava would be distraught, since the two of them had built up a friendship over his term. Grant ran inside and saw Ava on the couch, watching the news. Vanessa's death had been breaking news all morning and the story was still going strong. After listening several minutes to the news story, Grant picked up the remote and turned the television off. He sat next to his wife, hugging her as she cried.

"They didn't have to do that to her. Why, Grant? Why?" Ava sobbed, burying her face into her husband's shoulder.

"It's going to be all right, baby. They will find the people responsible for this soon enough. I will make sure this city doesn't sleep until justice is brought to this case."

He was upset as he thought about the bright future she'd had ahead of her and about her body in her apartment, just lying there dead.

"It doesn't make sense, honey. Why do people have to be so cruel?" she asked, just as Zach came downstairs from his room into the living room where his parents were sitting.

"I heard the bad news. Are you guys okay?" he asked.

"We'll be fine, son. Please make your mother some tea. I have a few phone calls to make, and I need to get ready to make a statement to the press regarding Vanessa," Grant responded.

"Grant, do me a favor and make sure justice is served. If we don't do anything else in our lives, we owe this to Vanessa," Ava said and Grant agreed.

The Lawyer's Office...

Jalen pounded his fist on his attorney's desk when he heard the bad news. The police had been there and intercepted his check with a warrant. All his lawyer said was they told him Jalen was wanted for questioning in a murder case. It was apparent that whoever had framed him before was up to their old tricks again. But why free him if they were just going to do this again to him? The only difference was he was now facing a life bid, and if whomever had their way, this time he would be serving the rest of his life in a prison cell for a murder he hadn't committed.

Jalen stormed out his attorney's office and got in his truck. He couldn't reach out to Taylor for assistance because there was some things that had been said at Olivia's house which led him to believe his wife may have known he was being set up the first time. He thought it had to be her and her father who'd concocted this plan. He wondered, if she hated him that much, why hadn't she just left him?

Then he wondered if it was all about the money. The church paid Taylor over two hundred fifty thousand dollars a year for handling the church's business. She was the bread winner in their marriage, and he would be entitled to alimony. But how were the pastor and his daughter connected to Grant's secretary? There was only one person who could help Jalen out of this mess, and that was Grant Ashford.

He had an alibi for last night, but he was sure Maurice wouldn't come forward. He was newly-promoted to sergeant, and certainly, he didn't want to mess that up. Plus, the governor seemed to have friends in high places. He could have Maurice fired in a heartbeat.

There was no choice left, so he picked up his phone and dialed Grant Ashford's number. Grant had a city-issued cellphone, along with a personal phone; hopefully, the number was still the same. To his surprise, Grant Ashford answered.

"Please don't hang up; I need to speak to you," Jalen said.

Grant caught the voice right away. He had made it to his office and was just about to call Walter so he could get his people involved and help find justice for Vanessa.

"Jalen, is this you?"

"Yes, it's me, and we need to talk, like a 9-1-1 conversation."

"I'm in my office."

"I can't come to the city-County building; that place is swarming with police."

"So what? You're a free man now. You can go anywhere you want—at least if it isn't a condition of probation or parole—and you aren't on either of them, if my memory serves me correctly," Grant said, wondering why Jalen was afraid of police interaction.

"Your memory? Wow, so it *was* you who got me released. Well, thank you and I appreciate you for doing that, but they are looking for me in connection with your secretary's death. Again, another crime I didn't commit. Why am I a pawn in some big chess game? I have no idea what's going on, but this time someone is trying to end the game with a checkmate."

Grant knew he was right about that. Walter had said some things last night after they made love that coincided with what Jalen was saying. Grant had had the feeling Walter was going after someone; however, he hadn't known the pawn was Jalen. But murder? Would Walter go this far?

"Okay; meet me at the spot where we first met up," Grant said, speaking in code just in case his phone was tapped. He had watched *Enemy of the State* too many times to trust even his own people.

"I'll be there in ten minutes," Jalen said and disconnected the call.

Grant made a call to Walter, who didn't answer and was probably in a meeting. He left a message for Walter to call him when he was free. There was one more person Grant knew he could trust. He looked at the phone and dialed his nephew in Ohio, who worked for the FBI.

Chapter 17

Walter Burke sat behind his desk with his brother, Pastor Burk, in front of him in one chair and Michael Addison in another chair. The three men hadn't been in the same room together since they were young boys.

"Things are going as planned. Grant isn't quite cooperating, but today he will find out what happens to people when they cross me. When he sees the video I have in my possession, I am quite sure he will be persuaded to do whatever I say," Walter said.

"I don't care about all the political stuff," the pastor retorted. "I just want this Jalen character out of the way *for good!"*

"Calm down. Indeed, my brother, your wish is my command. I appreciate you getting that tracker placed on Jalen's truck for me. Now I just need you to keep those envelopes coming to help fund my cause. That little niece of mine will be free as a bird within the next twenty-four hours. I'm sure her new-and-improved love, John, will be just as happy as you will be," the governor said.

Then he turned toward Michael, and instantly, his eyes were fueled with anger.

"I'm very disappointed in you, Addison! Jalen was your target three years ago when you visited Detroit, but just like now, you've allowed your heart and your foolish obsession with being in love to get in the way. You were supposed to lure him away from Detroit, get him away from Taylor. After that, I said I wasn't dealing with you anymore, but I gave you another chance by getting you the head coaching job here to handle *MY* business, and here you are crushing like a schoolboy again. You were specifically told *not* to start a relationship, Michael!

"Because of you and your insubordination, we've had to murder a Detroit police officer, because he would have been the alibi that Jalen couldn't have committed the murder. See, when I do things a certain way, there is always a reason. Didn't you say you wanted to make commissioner for the league? Well, I have a problem helping you get that position, *SINCE YOU'RE AN INCOMPETENT FUCK WHO CAN'T FOLLOW FUCKING ORDERS!*"

"Hold up, Walter, man, it ain't like that. You knew this shit would be hard for me. Billy is a great man, and with his money and talent, he would make a great addition to the boys' club,"

Coach said, trying to defend himself and make light of his screw up.

"THAT ISN'T THE POINT! I've been working this angle for over twenty years, and it's a shame that certain individuals like you and that last muthafucka I put in power just can't follow directions. I got him a job running the city, and he became an alcoholic who decided to get caught stealing the budget money and fucking his secretary. See, I know Grant's disposition and I know he won't go bad that way. I dealt with his father a long time ago, so I know what cloth Grant is cut from. You fucked this up back in his college days, and it's taken me years to get him back on track.

"Look, gentlemen, I'm not doing anything that hasn't been done by white folks. They groom their president from birth, instilling certain character traits in him to ensure that when the time comes, they will have the ability to place him in office and have it run accordingly. I just felt it was time for our kind to outsmart the system as well by creating our own network. All everyone has to do is follow my lead. We are eight years away from making history."

"My fault, man; I apologize," Michael said.

"Kids do dumb shit like that, and you're lucky that's all I want to say right now. I'm making the necessary calls to get Mundane traded. You'd better be glad I like you and still have use for you; otherwise, you would be out of a job and on your own. Don't forget I own a lot of shares in that team."

Michael lowered his head because he knew he had fucked-up again. He wasn't as powerful as Walter or his brother, but he'd wanted to play in the big leagues with them ever since they were kids. They had all grown up together, but Michael's family had moved him away when he was fourteen, after his father had caught him about to have a sexual tryst with two boys in their family's garage. Walter and Pastor Burk were those two boys.

Chapter 18

Grant sat by the Detroit River at Belle Isle Park, waiting for Jalen to arrive. He tossed rocks into the water, watching them skip four-to-five times across the cold waves before they sank and disappeared. He loved to come here to find peace. The island is totally surrounded by water, with one way on and one way off. He tried to think about the good times he'd spent with Jalen, but his head was fucked-up from the conversation he'd had with his cousin. Grant decided to call Walter, who answered and started talking before he could speak.

"Hello, Grant. I just sent you a text message."

"Sorry, I haven't received a message, but we need to talk about something. The police think Jalen Ross killed Vanessa, but he didn't do it."

"I know," Walter snidely responded.

"*You know?* So, *you* did this? Who murdered my secretary and why would you do this?"

"Why? Because you're sloppy! Never undo anything I have done. I told you before, I don't play checkers; I play chess. Every move I make is calculated and for a reason. There is a method to my madness. Her blood is on your hands, and the video in the text message I sent you will show you who."

"Video? Video of what?"

"Check your messages," Walter replied.

Just as he finished his statement, Grant received a text alert. Grant quickly tapped the notification and saw surveillance video footage of his son Zach parking and getting out his car on what looked like the same street as Vanessa's condo. Then the video switched to Zach on surveillance video in the condo lobby, then in the elevator. Grant was in total disbelief, holding the phone in silence. How on earth had Zach gotten wrapped up with Walter?

"Walter! I can't believe you! Are you saying *you had my son* kill Vanessa?!" Grant inquired, with the sound of pain and disbelief in his voice.

Walter laughed heartily and replied, "I didn't have your son do anything. This was all his idea. See, Zach has what it takes to become a great politician."

"But what about Jalen? Why would you mess up an innocent man's life like this?"

"Jalen messed up his own life by sticking his dick in my niece, but he sealed his fate when he stuck it in you. But you can save him *again* if you like, since you like saving people. You have the video. Turn it over to the authorities."

"So, save Jalen by turning in my own son? What kind of chess game is this? Do you think I'm a knight that you can simply toy with by moving me back and forth across your board?

"A knight?" Walters laughed. "You think too highly of yourself, Grant. You're a fucking pawn."

Walter ended the call just as Jalen pulled up. Grant walked toward him, when suddenly they both heard the police sirens. Jalen knew there was nowhere to go unless he jumped into the Detroit River. His eyes began to fill with tears.

"What the fuck, Grant?! Did you set me up?"

"No! I swear I didn't. It must have been Walter."

"Walter?! You told him where we were meeting?" asked Jalen, sounding defeated.

"No!"

Grant looked at his phone, realizing Walter must have tracked him. The red flashing lights were quickly approaching, and Jalen dropped to his knees and put his hands behind his head. The officers got out the car with guns drawn.

One yelled toward Grant, "MR. ASHFORD, ARE YOU OKAY?"

"Yes, I'm fine," Grant mumbled as he observed them roughly handcuffing Jalen, snatching him from his knees, and leading him to a squad car. Grant's phone vibrated in his hand just as he observed an officer removing a green Michigan State baseball cap and brown leather bomber jacket from the back of Jalen's truck, just like the one's Zach was wearing in the video.

Grant was devastated. The only way to prevent an innocent man from spending the rest of his life in prison was to tell the truth. He sighed just as he received a text alert on his phone. Grant looked at his phone and there was a message from Walter...

CHECKMATE!

Low Down Definitions

Low Down: information.
Example: What's the low down on Bobby and Whitney?

Low Down: despicable.
Example: Chandler is a low-down, dirty dog.

Down Low: secret.
Example: We can see each other, but let's keep it on the down low.

Down Low: men who secretly have sex with men without their wives or girlfriends knowledge.
Example: Ben and Ronald have been on the down low for years.

EXCERPTS FROM

THE APPLE DON'T FALL FAR FROM THE TREE

AND

LOW DOWN 2

The Apple Don't Fall Far From The Tree

The walls in my house were super thin, and I was sick and fucking tired of hearing the porn show going on night after night. Forget learning about sex from my responsible parents or from sex education at school, I got an up-close-and-personal audio show almost every day of the week except for when her nasty ass was on her period, and I'm sure she fucked through that half the time. The man's voice drifted in my room and I felt violated the way the nasty words swirled around my mind and body.

"Work that ass the way daddy likes it, bitch!" His grunts were disgusting and continuous. "Come on, bitch, work this big dick."

She was such a low-budget hoe. I didn't know much, but I knew from watching TV and listening to love songs that having sex was supposed to be loving and tender, not someone grunting out instructions and calling you a bitch.

"I told you to work that ass, bitch! Why you slowing down?" the man asked in a rough voice laced with attitude.

"I'm good, baby. I'm just enjoying this dick. Don't worry, mama's got you."

The sound of her voice alerted me that she was worn out. If she knew what was good for her, she would keep doing what she was doing, and not get her ass beat as she had done two weeks ago.

From the sound of the old, raggedy headboard being slammed into the wall and the joint escalated moans, I knew I would be able to get some peace and quiet soon enough. After a few more moments, I heard silence, then I heard heavy footsteps. Yes, they were done. The men never stayed to talk or anything. As soon as they came, they went.

I'm sorry. I'm telling you all about my issues, and I didn't even introduce myself. My name is Apple. I'm fifteen and in the tenth grade. My mother is the biggest hoe walking around Detroit, Michigan. That's right, I'm not talking about a neighbor who's sex crazed. I'm talking about my own mother, who knew I was lying in the very next room, listening to her suck dick and get her back knocked out day after day. My mother and I have a strained relationship, to say the least. Often times, I'm watching out for her, instead of the other way around.

When I was a lot younger, it was nothing for my mother to drop me off at my Big Mama's house for days at a time. Big Mama was my mother's mother and also my saving grace. She often said my mother didn't care about anyone but herself, and I use to get mad at Big Mama for saying that, but I've grown to agree with her.

It was fucked-up growing up feeling like I didn't belong anywhere because I was always getting dropped off here and there so my mother could party and get her freak on. She had fallen out with most of her friends, because either she would leave me with them too long and they got pissed off, or she was messing around with their husbands or boyfriends. My mother is a cold woman, and she doesn't give a shit who she screws over as long as she was getting some weed and or money.

The front door opened and closed, which was my cue to try to get a few hours of sleep before school. As soon as he left, I smelled the infamous smell wafting into my room. My mother was so predictable. As soon as she was done giving her body and self-worth to these men who didn't give a shit about her, she would sit on her bed and smoke weed until she fell asleep. She didn't give a damn that I had to go to school with my hair and clothes reeking of weed. I was teased to no end, until my cousins Nycee and Nicole gave me some big Ziplock bags to keep my clothes in, and I started tying my hair up at night. She could fuck her life up, but she wasn't about to have me being teased at school every day.

My cousins were a year older than me, and they resembled the celebrity twins Tia and Tamara Mowry. Most couldn't tell them apart, but I could with no problem. I resembled them, so we actually looked like triplets. Their mother was killed by their father when they were five, so they had been with Big Mama ever since. I envied them at times because at least they had someone looking after them who actually gave a shit.

I will say that one good thing came out of my mother's neglect and that was my skill to hustle. She never took the time with me a mother should with her child, so I'd had to teach myself how to cook, take care of myself, and do my own hair. I had even built me a nice clientele with some of the students at my school and other people around the neighborhood. The only problem with having people come to our house to get their hair done was it was really trying my luck because my mother didn't give a shit who was there. It was her house and she was going to do exactly what she wanted to do.

I'll never forget when Nycee was at a store and a woman asked her about her hair. She gave the woman my name and number. After making an appointment, the woman came over and I was so mortified because I knew my mother was in her room with a man. I blasted the TV to drown out the sounds coming from her room, and I thought we were all set. I finished her hair and I guess my mother finished her job at the same time, because right after the woman paid me, her husband walked out my mother's room with a big smile on his face and all hell broke loose.

I ended up having to call the Detroit Police. That was so embarrassing because all the neighbors started pouring outside, laughing and talking. By the time the police arrived, my mother had a busted lip and the woman's hair was a mess. She was screaming at the top of her lungs about how my mother had ruined her marriage. After all the chaos had settled down, my mother cursed me out for having the woman at 'her' house. Hell, I was trying to make money to put food in our house. How was I to know what was going on?

My thoughts were interrupted when my Metro PCS cellphone vibrated from under my pillow, and I saw it was my boyfriend Nicholas. Nick was three years older than me and out of high school.

"Hey, handsome," I whispered into the phone. My mother didn't know I had a cellphone and that's the way I wanted to keep it.

"What's up, babe? I know it's early, but I wanted to come by and get you for school. I need you to hold something at your house for me."

I sighed because I knew that meant he wanted me to stash some weed for him and that always made me nervous. Hell, I had enough bullshit to deal with when I was dealing with my mother. I wanted my relationship drama-free, but I couldn't turn him down.

"You know I got you," I said with confidence, but I really wasn't feeling it.

"That's my girl. I'll be there at seven, so be ready."

After we hung up, I decided to take a shower and get ready for school. I grabbed my toiletries and clothes, and I made my way to the bathroom. My mother must have heard me because her door flew open.

"Nick coming over here today?" she asked, looking me up and down.

"Yeah, he's taking me to school." I tried not to look in her eyes because she made me sick to my stomach.

"Good 'cause I need to get something from him. You'd better watch him, Apple, because I'm sure these little nappy-head girls be chasing after him. Don't get so busy doing hair that you forget to give Nick some attention. His fine, young ass probably gets pussy thrown at him all day long."

What kind of mother tells her daughter some silly shit like that? My mother had a lot of nerve acting as if I had to use my body to keep a man and get things. We lived in a small house in Brightmoor, an area on Detroit's west side, with old, shabby-ass furniture Big Mama had given us. She was on her back getting screwed on the daily, and she had nothing to show for it.

She didn't know it, but I'd overheard her talking to one of her fake-ass friends about me. She was saying how she'd gotten pregnant with me on purpose to trap my father into marrying her, but instead, he'd run the other way and never looked back.

"What do you need from Nick?" I asked as I scooted past her en route to the bathroom.

"Don't ask me what the fuck I need from him. Just make sure y'all don't leave this morning without me seeing him. I'm the mother, you're the child, so stay in your lane."

As I stood there talking to my so-called parental unit, the smell of sex drifted out her room like a dark, musty cloud. The mixture of sweat, weed, ass, and must swirled around me like a python. Before I could respond, she went back in her room and slammed the door. I was glad because I was sick of dealing with her and I needed to get ready for school.

After showering and putting on my clothes, I flat-ironed my shoulder-length, brown hair, and put a part down the middle. As I was smoothing out my hair, I heard Nick pull up. The sounds of the rapper Rick Ross were bouncing off the walls and our thin windows were vibrating. You would have thought he was picking my mother up the way she darted out the front door and ran to his truck. I peeked out the front window and was mortified when I saw her standing at the driver's side door, wearing a short nightgown with spaghetti straps barely holding her sagging C-cup breasts.

My mother was a very attractive woman with smooth brown skin, short, light-brown hair, a heart-shaped mouth, and alert almond eyes, and she was very curvy. I kept her hair in a short bob and she maintained it well. I often wondered why she chose to be so selfish. She didn't want to work for anything, except to open her legs in the V-shape.

I'd had enough of watching her make a fool out of herself outside, so I grabbed my book bag and walked to the passenger side of Nick's truck without even looking at her ass. When I got in, she had the nerve to smack her lips as though I was doing something wrong. Nick gave her a small plastic bag, and I was sure that was her weed supply for the next two days or so.

When we pulled up at my school, I saw most of the girls staring or trying to get Nick's attention. My mother's warning rang out in my head as I saw the attention Nick was getting. We hadn't had sex yet, but we had come pretty close. Nick had told me he would wait and he loved me, so he wasn't pressed. I gave Nick a kiss on the lips and went to look for my cousins. We always met up before first hour.

"Damn, your hair is gorgeous," Nicole said as they both walked up to me.

"Thanks." I smoothed out my already bone-straight hair and smiled.

"Girl, I started to call you last night because Big Mama is pissed with Auntie Tami."

I rolled my eyes because there was always drama when my mother was involved. "Really? What did my mom do now?"

"I heard Big Mama cursing her out because she borrowed some money and never gave it back. She was pissed off."

As we all talked and made our way to my locker, I realized I had forgotten my English report in my room. I snatched my cell phone out my pocket and called Nick. No answer. I called two more times. All three of my calls went to voicemail.

"Just turn it in tomorrow," Nycee said, smacking her gum, looking annoyed.

Any other time I would have, but I knew if I didn't turn that paper in, my grade would plummet. I was trying to get good grades so I could get into a good college, which meant I could get the hell away from my mother.

"I can't. I'm going to skip first hour, walk back home, and get it." The bell rang and we all parted ways.

Twenty minutes later, as I jogged down my street, my eyes squinted because I could have sworn I saw Nick's truck in my driveway. As I got closer, I saw that it was. This was confusing and very alarming. As I put my key in the front door, I knew my mother was fucking my boyfriend, and when I pushed the door open, there they were in the front room. Nick was sitting on the couch, and my mother was kneeling in front of him between his legs, sucking his dick like her life depended on it.

I stood there in total shock. Nick had his head thrown back on our old dusty couch, and my mother was as naked as the day her whore-ass was born. His dick was disappearing in her mouth, and she was bobbing her head up and down like she was listening to her favorite song. The scene was something out of a damn porno flick. I felt sick as she put his whole dick in her mouth and started licking his nut sack when she got to the bottom.

"YOU FUCKING BITCH!" I yelled, not being able to take it anymore.

They both jumped as if they had been hit with hot grease, and I was still stuck at the door. My feet felt like weights. My mother didn't even scramble around to get her clothes or cover up. She simply wiped her mouth with the back of her hand, stood up, and asked me what the fuck I was doing out of school.

At that very moment, I realized my mother had chased two men out of my life: my father and my first love. She was fucking poison.

I would forever remember what she said to me when she walked in front of me as Nick scurried to pull his pants up, *"A stiff dick has no conscience."*

Low Down 2

Jalen

Barely out of prison forty-eight hours and here I sit again in a cold, smelly jail cell. *This is fucking unbelievable!* All I wanted was answers. I know who, but I don't know why. Why would someone want to send me away for the rest of my life? Now, I know I've done some low-down, dirty shit in my life, but nothing to deserve life in prison.

I didn't murder that woman; I would never lay a hand on a woman. I watched my father do that to my mother for years. I think his abuse contributed to his death. My mother stood by him even though he made our lives a living hell, and he had the nerve to cheat on her. She was fed up and I was too. I had never even *met* Grant's secretary, so what reason would I have to kill her?

And now Maurice is gone. He was my alibi for Vanessa's murder and the only person who really had my back. The key to his house was still in my pocket when I was arrested, and my DNA was on his body and in his home. There was no way I was going to beat this. They say there's no such thing as a perfect crime, but hopefully, there's some evidence somewhere to prove my innocence. I can't believe I'm saying this but, God, if You're listening, I need You right now.

Zach

The key to playing chess is strategizing. To become a successful chess grandmaster, one must learn how to move their pieces off the starting squares and into the game rapidly. Your pieces will aid in your attack or your defense, and Walter was one of my pieces.

I knew Walter possibly was up to something when he started visiting me on campus, so I secretly videotaped him whenever he visited me to arrange his sexual escapades. I made sure he had different dates to select from every time. A scandal about the married governor participating in extramarital trysts with multiple young men sounds much better than him just sleeping with one man.

I love my father and I am willing to go to any means to protect him. I'll be by his side when he becomes mayor, and hopefully, he will be standing by my side when I become the new governor.

About the Author

For more than twenty years, Tonja Ayers has been helping women get on their feet by providing them with the latest trends in fashionable footwear. She has literally and figuratively provided the hottest styles in shoes, changing the fashion game and lives of women not only in Michigan but across the United States. Tonja has grown her business beyond selling dynamic shoes.

Affectionately known as "The Shoe Lady" worldwide, Tonja Ayers has made monumental strides in business, and she is also an author, publisher, playwright, and filmmaker. Following her passion for replaying life in the pages of books and plays, Tonja has mastered the process of taking the message from the page to the stage. She hosted her debut stage production, *Stay in Your Place*, to two sold-out performance theaters.

The success of the stage play inspired Tonja to begin developing scripts for films. Her first movie premiere sold out three movie theaters, with people standing in line for the next showing. In February 2020, Tonja released her second feature film, *Chocolate Kiss*, which premiered in five sold-out movie theaters. Her short film, *TEN*, has been nominated and selected for several film festivals. All of Tonja's books and movies are available on

Amazon as well as Tubi. Shoes are available at www.theshoelady.biz.

Made in the USA
Columbia, SC
30 May 2021

38612044R00130